The Kingdom of Heaven

The Kingdom of Heaven

*Eighty-Eight
Palm-of-the-Hand Stories*

John Gould

Ekstasis Editions

Canadian Cataloguing in Publications Data

Gould, John, 1959-
The kingdom of heaven

ISBN 1-896860-06-0

I. Title.
PS8563.08446K56 1996   C813'.54   C96-910596-7
PR9199.3.G6534K56   1996

© John Gould, 1996
Author Photo: Sandy Mayzell
Cover Art: Alanna Wood.
All rights reserved.

Acknowledgements:
Some of the stories in this collection have appeared previously in *Event, Geist,* and *Grain,* and in the chapbook *Misterioso,* published by Reference West for the Hawthorne Society of Arts and Letters. Thanks to Rhonda Batchelor, Charles Lillard, Robin Skelton, and the Hawthorne Society, for their support.

Thanks also to sympathetic, long-time readers, especially to Sandy Mayzell, Anne Louise Gould, Alanna Wood, Jane Fairbanks, and Marcia Williamson, for their ideas and encouragement. Thanks finally to Richard Olafson, for believing in the work and seeing it into print.

The expression *palm-of-the-hand story* was coined, so far as I know, by Yasunari Kawabata, from whom I gratefully borrow it.

Published in 1996 by:
Ekstasis Editions Canada Ltd.
Box 8474, Main Postal Outlet
Victoria, B.C., V8W 3S1

Ekstasis Editions
Box 571
Banff, Alberta T0L 0C0

The Kingdom of Heaven has been published with the assistance of a grant from the Canada Council and the Cultural Services Branch of British Columbia.

This book is dedicated to my loving parents,

Joan Anne and George Gould,

and to the memory of my maternal grandmother,

Frances Fulford,

who gave the great gift:
the gift of attentiveness,
the gift of attention.

Tya tum, tya ta tum,
Tya tum, ta tya tum.

        Glenn Gould
        (humming Sibelius,
        Symphony No. 5)

Contents

Devotion	9
China	10
Fruit	11
Pieces Of Glass	13
Woman With Necklace	14
Gaze	16
Cassiopeia	17
El Prado: A Novel	18
Desastres De La Guerra	20
How One Becomes Lonely	21
The Well-Tempered Clavier	23
Sleeper	24
Warm Milk	25
Cutty Sark	26
Second Draft	28
The Kingdom Of Heaven	29
The Destruction Of Knowledge	30
Fiction	32
Ultramarine	33
Aside	34
Hum	35
Snow	37
The Living	38
Triptyque: Imagining Mallarmé	39
Prayer	42
Experience	43
Field Trip	45
Piece	46
News	47
Park Bench	49
Out	50
Preface	52
Spree	54
Untitled LXIX	55
Synonyms	56
Watching Her Go	57
Desert	59
Kevin	60
Third World	61
Speak	62
Damage	64
Lipstick	65
Dear Pitiful	67
The Tower	68

Ocean	70
Despair	71
Facts Of Life	72
New Man	73
My Dad	75
Possession	76
Nothing Received	78
Babe	79
What She Asked Me	80
Wool	81
Misterioso	82
Smoked Salmon	83
Stab	84
What To Do Next	85
Session	86
Eddy	87
Ketchup	88
Violence	89
Look At Me	91
Cut Off	93
April	94
A Little Paradox	95
Revision	96
Weather	98
Stranger	99
Second Person	100
The Scientific Method	101
Block	102
A Third Thing	103
Crush	104
Speed Of Light	105
Yors	106
Mine	107
Leaving	108
The Art Of The Fugue	109
Codeine	110
Powaqa	111
Part	112
Pulp Fiction	113
Salad	115
Corpus	116
Rubber	117
All Possible Worlds	118
Picnic	119

Devotion

She was alight when I first saw her, through the glass there with all the other burning babies. She wasn't what I'd expected—I can say this now because I adore her, because I'd die for her. Her head was coned, crested with the shoving her mother had done before they opened her up. Her face was scrunched, alien. And of course there were the flames.

It's strange how startled I was—I'd been a burner myself, as my mother fondly tells it. Many babies are. You just put them out and get on with it. Still, it's a shock, I suppose, when you go looking for a sweet little bit of a thing and come upon a creature there, flickering madly like some crimson-shot opal. It takes you aback.

Amazing how quickly they learn, though. It hasn't been a year and she rarely blazes up now. I'm not saying there aren't incidents: we keep her away from the flammables, and from the good sofa set. But she understands, without the words to grasp it, that this can't go on. I get no pleasure from it, but I do what must be done: I starve her of oxygen and fuel, I put her to bed. Better now than later, as everyone reassures me.

Yet there are times I worry, times I wonder. Who, after all, am I cooling her down for? Who is it that'd be so troubled by her crackle and spark? Life's a little simpler, to be sure, if you're not forever flaring up like a Roman candle. Perhaps I'm doing her a favour. But I think back, way back to the days I myself was being tenderly tamped out. I think of my mother and father, the heartbreaking devotion with which they doused me, and it's not only gratitude I feel.

China

He says to me, Gina, it's a contradiction in terms, an oxymoron, *Christian marriage*. What's marriage, he says to me, what's marriage but a procreative contract, he actually says this to me, to his girlfriend of four years, a *procreative contract*, the purpose of which is to perpetuate the world, to prolong the abomination that is the world.

Walter, I say to him, what the hell are you talking about?

Gina, he says to me, Christianity is one thing, one thing only, it's the repudiation of the Judaic, which is to say the repudiation of family, of continuity, of temporality, he says to me. The goal of Christianity, he says to me, the goal of the Christian is to bring about an end to history by refusing to pass on the seed of selfhood.

Seed of selfhood, Walter? I say to him. Seed of selfhood? I'm asking you to help me pick out a china pattern, Walter. Jesus Christ.

The goal is to loathe china, Walter says to me. The goal is to loathe china and to love God.

Walter, I say to him, you're not as much fun as you used to be.

In truth I'm more fun, he says to me, in truth I'm far more fun. The ultimate fun is to do the will of God, and the will of God is to *stop the world*, he says to me.

Stop the world, Walter? I say. God made the world so that we could stop the world, Walter? God made human beings so that we could annihilate ourselves? And anyway, I thought you loved children.

Creation is a creation of irony, he says to me. Creation is meant to drive us from creation, he says to me. That's the whole point.

Walter, I say to him, let me ask you one thing. Let me just ask you one thing. Do you want your great-uncle Harry to sit up at the head table with us, or at a table with Anna? I'm serious now. Mom wants to know.

Christianity, he says to me, is the denial of the denial of spirit. Christianity is celibacy, he says to me.

Walter, I say to him, what are you saying to me?

The Kingdom of Heaven 10

Fruit

It's your own fault, truth be told. No one to blame but yourself. You were the artistic one ("autistic" is how you said it), especially at the time you were laden with him, loaded with him. Harmless way of handling that about-to-erupt feeling. Vases bristling with cut flowers, that sort of thing. Picture your hand, stained indigo, ochre, vermilion, resting on your great white bulging belly. It's tempting, is it not, to believe that a little of that colour seeped through the blank page, burst into his vision before he was ready?

Yes, but this? Can this be art? It's the first time he's had a piece in a gallery, a legitimate gallery—you'll be kind to him if it kills you. But this? No paint, just the two round photos hanging like fruit from a trunk of text. *Jerking Off*, he's called the thing. Jesus. To the left, a photo of a painting: Guido Reni's "Saint Sebastian". Young man hung from a tree, torso bristling with arrows. To the right, a photo of a photo of the author Yukio Mishima posing as Guido Reni's Saint Sebastian. Between them, a wooden panel on which is splashed in red ink (you recognize your son's shaky hand):

"The arrows have eaten into the tense, fragrant youthful flesh...." The young man, martyred, bearing witness, begs the young man to bear witness to his martyrdom. The young man, the poet, the seer, is penetrated by the image of the young man penetrated, body bursting, seed spilling for the first time over the image of the body burst. Sweet silken skin punctured, releasing the death held in all his life, the life dammed up in his dying body. Hot fluid hungry for escape. Boundary broken, the one moment of truth. Inner bleeding into outer. Self into other. A young man bearing witness to this truth, to a young man bearing witness to this truth. Begging you to bear witness to this truth as he bears witness, escapes....

Jesus. Is this what's on his mind all the time, all those times he says nothing? Is this what fills that beautiful head, the head that sets all the other boys' beautiful heads spinning? The head so brilliant and brimming even on that first day—twenty-five years ago now—that it refused to emerge from between your legs? After all the groaning and shrieking, your belly slashed....

Seppuku. That's what they call it in Japan, as you recall. The way Mishima went, as a matter of fact, twenty-five years ago—shocking the world, a world incited to watch—slitting his belly to let his own life splash free....

"Mom?"

Picture him in your hands, hot and tiny, sweet with your womb's water. The sudden sense of *danger*.

"Mom?"

Turn to him, slowly, carefully, a ripe fruit afraid of bursting.

Pieces Of Glass

I only ever go to openings for the wine and the mini quiches, the beautiful women posing in front of paintings, hipshot, sweetly frowning, beautiful heads tilted a little this way or that, so busy staring as to be oblivious to your stare. You stare at them, they stare at the painting, everybody's happy. I'm not an art person, I know what I like and it isn't art. I like women, I like food, I don't like art. Art doesn't do a thing for me, or didn't at least until the opening last week, same as usual, wine and mini quiches, but there was something about the art, about the paintings. I can't say. One minute I was staring at this woman who was staring at a painting, a beautiful woman, they're all beautiful in my books but this one, honestly, she was something to stare at, and the next minute I was staring at the painting she was staring at. Maybe it was her staring itself that took my eyes with it, if you see what I mean, something about her stare, the way she was staring, and all of a sudden I was staring with her at the painting. I did this for quite a while, stood staring with her at the painting, and then I turned and walked away, walked over to where the artist with the little name-tag was standing by the mini quiches, shovelling them in, nervous I suppose, and I said, "I want that painting. It'll go nicely with my couch," though this was a lie. I knew even then that it would clash.

"Oh," she said.

I said, "How do you do it? How do you do such paintings?"

She said, "They just sort of come out, you know? It's like—" She stopped, thought a moment. "It's like, I had this car accident? My shoulder was full of glass, these pieces of glass? And the doctor wouldn't take them out, they were too deep, and he said just to wait, that my body would push them out, like, in its own time? And it did?"

And I wanted, just then—as you can perhaps imagine—wanted more than anything, more even than I'd wanted the wine or the mini quiches, to see that skin, that scarred skin where the glass had gone in, where the glass had come out, to touch it, taste it, and I did, on the couch beneath the painting, after we'd hung it there, the two of us, the artist and I. It was beautiful, that scarred skin, the most beautiful part of that beautiful woman, the most beautiful perhaps of all the world's beautiful women, though of course who can ever say that for sure? I haven't seen her since that night, my artist, but I have the painting now to stare at, when I'm alone, this strange painting, this oddly shaped shard of glass that takes all my staring and turns it around, somehow, reflects it, gives it back to me, almost as though it were me, as though I were the beautiful one.

Woman With Necklace

"It's a Modigliani," she says. "Do you know him?" She shakes her head. "I mean, you don't *know* him, obviously. He's *dead*." She shakes her head again. She's almost as bemused as he is—dating again after all these years. She sips her wine, nods at the framed print hanging above her overstuffed chair, across the room from the couch upon which the two of them so uneasily perch. "Do you like it?" she says.

"Yes," he says. And then, as if after yet deeper rumination, "I do." No further comment suggests itself to him.

She tilts her head thoughtfully, gazing at the picture, in which a woman sits thoughtfully gazing out of almond-shaped eyes, oval head tilted slightly to one side atop a long, swan-like neck. He really does like the picture. Has he seen it before, or is it another Modigliani he's thinking of? Aren't they all a little like this?

"'Woman With Necklace,'" she says. She's a friend of a friend of his late wife's. A woman his age, two grown kids to match his three. Husband gone two years (heart attack) same as his wife (cancer). Perfectly natural. Time to move on, to start living again.

"But who is she really?" she says.

"Hmm?" he says. He sips his wine.

"This 'Woman With Necklace'. I don't mean who sat for the painting, who was his *subject*—that was Jeanne something-or-other, the woman who became his wife. What I'm wondering is, did she really have that long, swan-like neck? Did any of the women he painted actually have that long, swan-like neck? Maybe he was only interested in women with long, swan-like necks, maybe they're the only ones he'd agree to paint. Or maybe they all started growing long, swan-like necks the moment they met him, maybe their necks grew longer and more swan-like every hour they spent with him. Or maybe they never did...."

She lets her voice trail off: out of steam, presumably. He musters no reply. They sit silently gazing, the two of them, at the woman with the long, swan-like neck who sits silently gazing at them out of those almond-shaped eyes. Her necklace, a heavy chainlike affair, reminds him of a necklace he once bought his wife. He picked it out himself; she liked it. The subject's expression, too, seems somehow familiar. A peaceful loneliness. A luminous poise. Yet he can't just remember ever having seen it before.

"He died a few years later," she says. "Modigliani. A few years after this picture was painted. By the time his body was under ground she'd thrown herself out a sixth-story window, this Jeanne whatever. Why am I telling you this?"

She turns to him, swivels her head on what he'd have to describe, now that he takes note of it, now that he's looking, as a remarkably long, swan-like neck.

He stands up, abruptly. "I'm sorry," he intends to say, and head for the door. What he actually says, though, is, "Yes."

Gaze

You have his eyes, my mother used to say to me as a boy—wistfully, regretfully, even on occasion accusingly—as though I'd filched them from this mythological man, this trumped-up father, as though I'd scooped them from his skull and pressed them into my own empty sockets, blinded him in order to grant myself sight. Or as though perhaps he'd uprooted them himself from his manly brain, last thing before leaving, sown them in my head as he'd sown the seed of me in my mother's belly. Big brown eyes, beautiful I'm told—I recall my mother's sighs as I gazed at her gazing into them in me. A touch of green, of hazel. I imagine him (never having seen him, even an image of him), imagine him gazing out of those eyes into those eyes in me, preparing to leave. I gaze into my eyes in the mirror, into his eyes in me. I gaze into his eyes out of my eyes. Out of my eyes, in the mirror, I gaze into his eyes —nested now in a complexity of creases, bloodshot with lack of sleep, a new father's eyes—the eyes of a man who was able to look at me, to look into these eyes in me and to leave. I gaze into my young son's eyes—my eyes, his mother tells me, smiling, the mother who's given him her lips, by the way, her gorgeous lips—wondering with what eyes he sees me out of the eyes I see, my father's eyes, eyes which of course weren't my father's eyes at all but someone else's eyes before him. Eyes he saw in the mirror out of eyes we'll never see. I wonder what words he'll fashion with those lips, my son, with his mother's lips, to let us know what we've failed to see in him, how much even of ourselves we'll never see in the face in the mirror, in the mirror of his face.

Cassiopeia

For so long I believed I ought to have one, to have a face, tormented myself for this lack, scorned and ridiculed myself for my facelessness. I required a face, couldn't possibly go on living without one. It's a dreadful predicament, as you must know, my sweet, to hold the desperate conviction that one must have what one can't have, to hinge one's worth, one's very existence on the possession of what can't be possessed: a face. It's so clear to me now. A face is something that can be seen, something that can't possibly be seen *out of*. To see *out of* a face, *out of* anything, would be perfectly, sickeningly absurd. To have a face would be precisely not to be yourself, but to be someone else. The trick of the mirror is that it leads you to believe you've seen yourself—the one thing which of course you'll never see—when in truth you've seen something wholly and hideously other. You've seen, at best, a shadow thrown, the shadow of a mask behind which are concealed your wonder and shame, shame at your irredeemable facelessness.

This is the shame I've lived with all these years, my sweet, which sadly led to the misery which drove you away. The shouting was...the shouting was detestable. You were right to leave, I'm not saying that. I'm not asking you to forgive, or to forget. It's only that I long for you, for the sight of your face, those strange dark eyes, the freckled skin across your cheeks, the uncanny curvature of your nose, most of all the little w-shaped scar above your lip, which reminds me, has always reminded me of Cassiopeia, the constellation named for the Ethiopian queen tossed up into the heavens for the sin of having fallen in love with what she saw in the glass.

You have no face, my sweet—of course you haven't. I understand. I'm not expecting....

Please, just see me again. Just see me.

El Prado: *A Novel*

Chapter One: *Consider Your Future*

The young man who's the protagonist of this story (which as you see has chapters, establishing beyond a doubt that it's a proper novel) went to Europe at the age of eighteen, just as his father had done. Frank Senior crossed the ocean in 1944, to find Hitler and kill him—Hitler beat him to it. Frank Junior followed him in 1974, to find himself—or lose himself, whichever came first.

"What?!" said his parents in unison.

Frank's parents spoke only in unison. The last time they'd spoken out of unison, as a matter of fact, was shortly after Frank Junior's birth. Frank Senior had demanded at dinner one night, "Are you sure that's all my sons, Doll? I'm still hungry!" "That's all of them!" Doll had sweetly replied, hiding young Frank, her favourite, in the folds of her apron.

Between them, now, they cried out to their only son, "Consider your future!"

Chapter Two: *She's A Lesbian*

"It's okay Mom, Dad," said Frank Junior. "I'll be back in six months and I'll go to school. I'll become a journalist and have an interesting life with my half-Japanese wife, Mariko, and our quarter-Japanese children, Frank and Bonzai." (All of which will come about, though Bonzai will be known simply as Bonnie.)

"But you'll be so terribly alone!" said his parents.

"Actually, I'm taking Joanna with me," said Frank Junior.

"A girl!" they cried in horror.

"It's okay Mom, Dad," said Frank Junior. "She's a lesbian."

Chapter Three: *A Sweet Sticky Red Good Time*

Which was true, though in Frank Junior's case she made one exception. On the night of their arrival in Madrid, to be specific, their first night Abroad. They'd found themselves a little room in a *pensión* overlooking a courtyard (a courtyard!) in which a clutch of dark-haired children hid and sought, and where brilliant laundry (laundry!) hung on a line. They were both so excited that they decided it would be absurd not to make love. This was Frank Junior's first time, however, and Joanna's first time with a body so different from her own, so that it took two bottles of sweet sticky red wine to get them into bed, where they proceeded to have a sweet sticky red good time.

Chapter Four: *The House Of The Deaf Man*

And awoke in the morning to sunlight pouring down out of a Spanish sky, the smell of coffee and bacon wafting up from a Spanish kitchen. After breakfast Frank and Joanna strode purposefully through Spanish Streets, past pairs of taut uniformed young Spanish men with guns cradled in their Spanish arms, to *El Prado*, which is the name of a big Spanish art gallery and of this little novel, both. And they strode past El Greco's elongated longing saints and past Velasquez' dour earthbound dwarves and past Goya's Majas—Naked and Clothed—and descended to the ground floor where the Black Paintings are housed, those burnt-sienna visions Francisco de Goya scrawled onto the walls of his hermitage, *La Quinta Del Sordo*: the House of the Deaf Man.

Chapter Five: *Something Was Beginning*

And finally came to a stop before "Saturn Devouring One Of His Children", a smallish painting which made Joanna shudder, and mutter the word, "Chiaroscuro," though she couldn't recall just precisely what that meant.

And Frank Junior gazed at the demented god, with his long dishevelled grey hair, his wide eyes mad with fear and ambition, his gaping mouth, and at the dangling half-devoured body of one of his spawn.

"Dad?" he said.

And he knew that something was at an end—this novel—and that something was beginning.

Desastres De La Guerra

Napoleon's in the Pyrenees, quaffing the white cold air, cleansing his palate for another banquet of blood and bone. In the south Goya awaits him. His preparations are complete. The copper plates and trenchant tools of intaglio are readied and laid by, the special ink, equal parts earth and tears, smouldering darkly in its sealed bottles. Images hover in the air about him, adumbrations of what's to come: glinting curve of steel, roundness of flesh severed and spoiling, dark ellipses of howling mouths. There's no time now for prayer, even to his own divided heart—time only for supplication to the muse. *Let me die slowly of my wounds. Let my blood pool in black visions. Let madness hold me awhile before crushing me in its long arms....*

But he sees her lifted, already, his scowling sorceress, hoisted from a cart heaped with rigid refuse, skirts rucked up around her waist, and heaved into the dank mass grave. This is what he has, in fact, always seen; this is his imagination ruptured and running loose on the world. A great shudder is set off within him, a roiling of rage and shame....

He hunches forth over his first plate, stylus delicate between trembling fingers, to take the first blow.

How One Becomes Lonely

So in this scene you'll be brooding over a score at your desk in Traunkirchen, as for that matter you'll be brooding over one score or another in every blessed scene of this blessed film, at your desk in Traunkirchen, at your desk in Mödling or in Vienna, at your desk in Berlin or for that matter at your desk here in Hollywood. This film is nothing, nothing whatsoever but a succession of scenes of brooding, of you brooding over one score or another at one desk or another, as you know perfectly well, since of course this is the life of Schoenberg that stirs me, the life of genius that stirs me, that stirs a genius like me. The creative life. No quaint childhood scenes, no schmaltzy love scenes. No sweaty, swoony performance scenes. Nothing but creation scenes, brooding scenes. Jesus. These creeps, these Hollywood cretins won't know what's hit them. One hundred and eleven minutes of creation. One hundred and eleven minutes of brooding, one hundred and eleven minutes of you sitting there at your desk. They won't fucking believe it.

So as I say, in this particular scene you'll be brooding at your desk in Traunkirchen, Austria. I just want to go over it one more time, okay? So you know just exactly how you're brooding, how Schoenberg would have been brooding. You're in between the two wars. You're a Lutheran Jew. You've taken Jesus as your saviour, but you know it won't do you any good, that you'll soon be just as homeless as every other Jew in Europe. You've been baptised, but won't pander to them by proving it. You've yet to write your little essay, *How One Becomes Lonely*, but your research is coming along nicely. You've passed through your late-Romantic phase, left behind your Wagner on the one hand, your Brahms on the other, left behind the whole tonality thing, the whole concept of a tonic, of a tonal centre to any given composition. A home. You've been out there in the wilderness of atonality for a while, of pantonality, where all notes are equal. Where anything goes. Where dissonance prevails, a dissonance that's no mere waiting for resolution but life itself. A resolution infinitely postponed. Where only the faintest whiff of a key signature remains, a melancholy reminiscing—reminiscing most of all about D minor, your beloved D minor....

We'll get all that later. What we're going for right now is the moment, the key moment at which your new method of creating, your new mode of brooding is emerging from this chaos. The *tone row*, they'll call it, your disciples, the sequence of notes that'll be your new skeleton, the new form on which to feed your flesh. The new justification for all those flights of fancy. The new set of fetters that'll give you back your freedom. Okay? The new rigour that'll set you loose, the new logic in which you'll lodge your faith. Okay? The new head blooming in your heart, to match the new heart blooming in your head. Okay? In your balding head. You'll run your hand over your head, just like this, over your balding head—we'll shoot it from above, right, Ben?—pick up your pen and go back to brooding over your score, which as you know is the score of the last of the *Five Piano Pieces, op. 23*. The waltz. Your first piece based purely on a tone row, C #-A-B-G-A*b*-G*b*- B*b*-D-E-E*b*-C-F, and of course its myriad mirror images. There'll be no sound, no sound for one hundred and eleven minutes—they won't fucking believe it—but the scratch of your pen, an occasional sigh, a sigh of joy at the beauty of this new structure, this new way of structuring. A rush of blood through your new body of bone....

    Okay? Got it?
    So start brooding.
    And...*action*.

The Well-Tempered Clavier

We're at the same concert, Del and I, in the same concert hall, listening as the same pianist picks out the intricacies of Bach's composition, but we listen differently, Del and I, she constructively, if you will, I destructively. I'm in my good grey suit, she's in her maroon blouse and beige skirt. She listens constructively, I destructively, if you will. It's in her nature to begin from complexity and move towards simplicity, while it's in my nature to begin from simplicity and move towards complexity. Our hands are linked, my right in her left, fingers interlaced; from time to time one of us accents a note or chord by tapping it out on the back of the other's hand. The various threads of the fugal structure interlace, subject and answer, subject and subject inverted, augmented, diminished, made retrograde, two, three, four separate voices. It's in Del's nature to hear distinct voices and from them fashion a whole, if you will, while it's in my nature to hear a coagulation of voices and tease them apart. Del is multiplicity longing for integrity, I'm integrity longing for multiplicity, if you will. Del's multiplicity derives from the experience of having had her head banged against door frames quite frequently as a child, cigarettes butted out on the soft skin of her thighs, skin which is now, nonetheless, of such delicate perfection as to perfectly defy description. Del speaks in many voices and longs to speak in one voice, if you will, I speak in one voice and long to speak in many voices. She listens in order to conjure a self, I in order to shatter a self, if you will. Shortly, at intermission, we'll shuffle out into the lobby with the other suited, skirted patrons, and we'll stand together, hand in hand, listening.

Sleeper

I *love the child*, I say to myself, meaning that I love living in the presence of this proposition, that I *love the child*, love holding it, holding it to be true. It's true that I love the child in the sense that it's true that I love loving the child. I love being in this condition, the condition of loving the child, which is the condition of loving loving the child. I long for the child, yes, long to hold it, which is to say that I lack the child even when I hold it. To hold the child would be to give up longing for the child. To hold the child would be to enter into a condition of total absurdity, to enter into the faith that I'm real, so real as to be capable of holding the child, that the child is real, so real as to be capable of being held. To enter into this faith would be to love. *To enter into this faith would be to love*, I say to myself....

The child in its sleeper stirs against my shoulder. Some dream, some hunger. A warm puddle of drool gathers in the cup of my collarbone, drains away.

Warm Milk

It has nothing to do with believing in God but with giving yourself to God, or rather with giving *myself* to God, putting myself in God's hands. Belief has nothing to do with it. Believing keeps me awake, not believing keeps me awake, what's the difference? Only giving myself to God allows me to sleep, putting myself in God's hands. This is the only way I've ever slept, personally, on those rare occasions when I have in fact *slept*, as opposed to lying here stewing, lying here between the sheets in a *stew*, as I'm doing just now, for instance. It's not possible to sleep, to close your eyes and as it were to *blink out of existence* without first of all giving yourself to God, putting yourself in God's hands. How else could you possibly sleep? This is the only way I've ever slept, myself, the only way I've ever been able to blink out of existence, by first of all giving myself to God, putting myself in God's hands. This became clear to me last night, just as I *drifted off*, as I *let myself go*, that I'd first of all unconsciously given myself to God, put myself in God's hands, and that only this first step had made sleep feasible for me, that only this first step had ever made sleep feasible for me. This realization changes everything. I lie here now, as you see, stewing, not over the question, *How do I sleep?* but over the question, *How do I give myself to God, how do I put myself in God's hands?* These amount of course to the same question—this I'd never realized until last night, by which time I'd of course already given myself to God, put myself in God's hands. How did I do it? Why can't I do it now?...

Perhaps some warm milk. Or perhaps if you told me a story, about a puppy, say, a happy little puppy as sweet and pure as if he'd never woken up at all.

Cutty Sark

Once upon a time there was—
We've heard it, Dad. Jesus Christ.
Mind the lip, kiddo. Okay, so in the beginning was—
Ah, pull the other one, Dad.
For God's sake. All right, and then you'll shut up and sleep?
Of course we'll sleep. We'll be soothed.
We'll be comforted.
Wiseacres. Pair of wiseacres. Okay, so there's this man, see, kind of a lumpy, middle-aged type of a man, likes his Cutty Sark, and his wife's up and left him, a great woman, understand, but with this hankering for, you know, to find herself, so the man, he's left with his two boys, two fantastic kids mind you, but they're insomniacs, means they can't—
It's been done, Dad. Jesus Christ, read a book once in a while why don't you.
Dad, don't leave. Come on, he didn't mean it.
The hell he didn't. Look, I could use a drink anyways. Good night, boys.
No, he's right. I didn't mean it. Honest.
It's just that.... Dad, don't leave.
Okay, okay, nobody's leaving.
It's just that we're troubled. We, we're, we live in, you know, troubled times.
I understand that. I fully understand that.
So we need a story. We lack direction. We need...you know, for our, for what's going on with us.
It's about that drink, boys.
No, hang on. Just hang on a sec. See, a person's life...there's no *shape*....
Where do you kids *get* this kind of crap?
Dad, it's not crap. I'm trying to tell you—
You know, boys, when I was your age—
Dad, *please*—
No, listen. I mean it. Take this afternoon. I'm on my way home from work, I've had one or two, it's been a long day. I come up out of the subway and there's this kid standing there, I can't tell is it a boy or a girl, it has no hair, looks as though it's AWOL from some war, if I ever, *ever* catch you boys looking...all right, all right, so anyways, I'm thinking it's about to kill me, pull out a bayonet or something, they'll

do anything for drugs, and it looks at me out of these sunken, beaten up sort of eyes and says *everything is the case*. That's what it says, it says *everything is the case* about three times, and then it bashes the back of its head against the wall and starts crying. I mean, it just starts blubbering like some big ugly child. *Everything is the case.* Now for chrissake—

    Thanks a lot, Dad.
    Yeah, Dad, that was great. Perfect.
    Oh. Well, I guess I'm just trying to say that—
    It's okay, Dad. Really. Thanks a lot.
    Right. Well, good night then, boys.
    Yeah, good night, Dad.
    Good night.

Second Draft

The first line of the first draft of this story (entitled at that time *First Draft*) went, *To be seen is the ambition of ghosts, and to be remembered the ambition of the dead.* Pretty snappy, I thought, though a touch top-heavy. How was I to get from this dilly down into the *action*? The story was supposed to be about a voyeur, or rather about an exhibitionist, the willing object of a voyeur's attentions, and his need to be spied on in order to experience himself (clichéd gender roles were cleverly reversed in my story, the gazer a woman, the gazed-upon a man). This guy can't get it up, you see, until he's seen to be getting it up —my metaphor for the loss of authenticity in our culture, our compulsion to be viewed, to be made real by somebody else's vision. This man's a ghost, then, his striving for substance a metaphor in turn for his need to exist when he no longer exists, when he's dead and gone....

It was getting pretty complicated, to tell the truth. I thought I'd leave it a while, come back to it.

My boyfriend at the time, Lawrence—oh hell, Larry, he'll never read this—happened to be reading Norman O. Brown's book, *Love's Body*. He was reciting bits out loud to me, expounding on them at enormous length—he needed to be listened to, did Larry, to be convinced he had anything at all in his head. "Those for whom not to be seen is non-existence are not alive," he read to me one night, "and the kind of existence they seek, the immortality they seek, is spectral; *to be seen is the ambition of ghosts, and to be remembered the ambition of the dead.*"

Well, well, I thought to myself.

Larry'd already launched into his exegesis—bereft of irony, as usual, of any trace of self-awareness—but I cut him off.

"Have you ever read this to me before?" I asked him.

"No," he said. "Why can't you *listen*?"

It gave me a chill, to tell the truth. How did those words get from his book, Norman Brown's book, into mine? Was all writing perhaps part of one vast, intricately allusive text, in the course of which certain phrases might crop up repeatedly, in the manner of a refrain? If so, who was in a position to comprehend such a text?

This became the underlying theme of my second draft. Which I'm pleased with, on the whole, glancing it over, though it's awfully discursive, and short on sex. I'll have to spice it up in the third draft, I think, if I'm to get myself read.

The Kingdom Of Heaven

for A.L.

Glendy was about ready to draw the line. What with Graham's child support cheque bouncing, Andrew getting his tongue frozen to the goal post at school, Ernst the chameleon going belly up, Bangladesh under about a foot and a half of snake-infested water, the ozone layer oozing ultraviolets and the universe at large running downhill towards a state of maximum disorder and pointlessness, it seemed clear to her that someone would have to do it. Glendy asked around, but most of her friends were completely flummoxed by the question of where to draw the line, paralysed by the fear of drawing it in the wrong place. Her therapist expressed concern. "Do you often feel this urge to draw lines, Glendy?" he wondered. "No," said Glendy. "Did it ever bother you when your father drew the line?" "I'm not sure he ever drew it," said Glendy, fighting back tears. "Ah," murmured the doctor, "Ah." Graham, over the telephone, was his usual rational, querulous self. "But Gwendolyn, what is it to say that any particular line is *the* line? I mean, aren't there really an infinite number of possible lines? And if so, how can we claim an absolute veracity for the idiosyncratic geometry of our own...." Glendy broached the topic with her mother during one of their Sunday visits. With a wistful, it's-so-burdensome-to-be-right smile, Mrs. Williams said, "I guess I've never understood why you didn't draw it years ago, when we asked you to. Are you sure it isn't a little late now?" Andrew, looking on as Ernst bore deeper and deeper into the toilet's pine-scented vortex, was youthfully nihilistic. "Thell ith no line," he said. Glendy's lover, Suzanne, assured her that whichever way Glendy decided they'd always have one another. When Graham's cheque finally came through, Glendy made it over to a relief fund for refugees of the flood. On Saturdays, when Graham had Andrew, she began roughing out a work of fiction, a series, an edifice of fictions entitled *The Kingdom Of Heaven*, into which she intended to pour so much love and rage and knowledge that it would stem, perhaps reverse, the tide of entropy, the slow collapse of the cosmos.

Suzanne types and edits it on Sunday afternoons.

The Destruction Of Knowledge

I've made my decision—I've received my calling. I'm the man. What God needs of me now, what the Word most needs is an *editor*. I, Irenaeus of Lyon, will shoulder this burden just as my Saviour shouldered His—the gnarled rood—not two centuries ago, for my redemption and the redemption of all *true* believers. Amen.

In the amphitheatre today they flayed the skin from two more of our kindred, after first branding them with red-hot irons, then hung them from wooden posts to be disembowelled by the beasts. When a man's martyred for uttering the words, "I'm a Christian," he ought at least to have some idea what he's dying for. I'll tell him.

In a sense, the World doesn't yet exist. There's chaos, merely, a miasma of conflicting tales of a world that might come into being. Light must be divided from darkness, the sacred from the profane, orthodoxy from heresy. And so I find myself faced with compiling the Book of Creation, with all possible versions and perversions spread out before me. From this blizzard of fictions I must pluck reality; from all possible tales of the Christ I must winnow out the foolish and the false, until I'm left with Gospel.

Sometimes, I'm afraid, my heart fails me. Not that my discriminations can fail to be correct: God will guide my hand as it strokes out each word of demoniac delusion. Yet how is the mind of a righteous man to bear these abominations? Christendom draws the infidel to it even as the flame draws the moth. The barbarisms of Persia, Egypt, Babylon, of Jew and Zoroastrian, not to mention the whimpering of the Asian, the chilly syllogizing of the Greek, all seep in to poison the pure water of the Holy Spirit. Great are the forces that would reduce the message of God to a heathen babble, the Priesthood to a rabble of madmen, sorcerers, and women, the Church to a potboiler of satanic rites. *If those who lead you say to you, "See, the kingdom is in the sky," then the birds of the sky will precede you. If they say to you, "It is in the sea," then the fish will precede you. Rather, the kingdom is inside of you, and it is outside of you. When you come to know yourselves, then you will become known, and you will realize that it is you who are the sons of the living father....* Such are the gnostic blasphemies poured into the mouth of the Son of God. Let these aberrations be exorcised, let them simply be omitted from a single sanctioned text, and they'll rot as fruit that has dropped from the vine.

First my book then, first the blade. I entitle it, *The Destruction and Overthrow of Falsely So-called Knowledge*. What remains when ignorance has been slashed away will be quite simply the Book of God. It will consist of four voices, but one Truth, in the name of the one Father and His earthly Priesthood. He who hears it and believes will find salvation. He who hears it and disbelieves will go to hell.

Amen.

Fiction

The trick is to open with something absurd, some outrageous conceit that sucks them into your world. Something irrational that forces them into a position of *faith*. You dare them to disbelieve—they don't. They assent to that first ludicrous claim and you've *got them*. You've got a cockroach conversing, say, with a widow about the end of the world. You've got a monk making it with the Mother Superior. You've got a *man giving birth*, labouring six days to squeeze the universe out from between his ears.

They buy that, they'll buy anything.

Ultramarine

I was born, heaved free of that hot briny sea with a rack of gills on either side of my neck. They could hardly throw me back, so they hung me upside down and whacked me until I coughed and came forth onto land. Out of my ooze, out of the sweet murmuring silence of my sludge. If not for my dreams, my nightly descents into the dank ultramarine of an ancient past, I myself would long ago have forgotten. Yet right away she knew. From her great height, I suppose, she'd been keeping an eye out for the lost, the beached soul, for the telltale iridescence of its rot.

So I found myself, within hours of meeting Rosalind, back at her apartment on my back in the dim recesses of her bed, her harsh tongue lapping quizzically at the scars on my throat. My hands were full of her flesh, or rather, of her plumage: over her breast and belly was spread a mat of white down. A coarse, vestigial growth of flight feathers swept down her back and arms. Rosy rose up over me, swivelling her head, displaying the aquiline profile of her nose, the arch of her powerful neck, the full fathomless glare of her glassy eye. I entered her as the sea enters the sky, a mingling of blues at some distant horizon. What she uttered wasn't a moan, but a cry. She was a wild bird. This was her flight.

Sadly, since that night, love hasn't been so trouble-free for Rosalind and me. The simple truth is that we get on one another's nerves. She's forever plucking at her feathers, clacking her beak like a common crow; I flop around at night, chomping and rolling my eyes until it's all she can do not to club me. Beyond these mundane horrors of intimacy, it's proving difficult for us each to live with an exile. We share our expatriation, but not our homeland. Sometimes I fear it'll all end in violence. Summer days, while I frolic at the beach, steeping myself in my own cold blood, Rosy squats in the low gnarly branches of a cedar tree, glaring at me and tensing her scarlet talons, as though she'd like to swoop down and seize me up forever into her empty kingdom.

More likely, though, when the time comes, she'll go alone. There'll be a note, brief and tender, perhaps an empty vial. Often I wake up to see her perched on the window sill, blinking her beady eyes into the light, warming her feathers and bones as if in anticipation of some updraught powerful enough to carry her away. When it comes for her, at last, it'll be time for me too. Time to open up my roaring veins, draw myself a little sea and plunge into it.

Aside

It left the room only briefly, the narrative voice, with the intention of catching in a phrase or two the scent, sound, and sight of evening rain outside her window, each drop a tiny universe containing the big one—lights of distant stars and galaxies, mercury streetlamps, headlights, bic lighters—little worlds bursting apocalyptically against her glass, expiring, streaming down her pane like so many unwiped tears. The voice, the narrative voice had in mind connecting the falling of these orbs with the falling of her robe, as she stepped out of it bedside, freeing her body, freeing her pale torso with its milk-heavy orbs, freeing herself at last to touch herself as she's not been touched since the night her daughter was conceived, fantasizing perhaps about the father—that stranger—grown slightly less strange these ten months beneath her skin. But the voice is too slow, or she too sleepy, after a day of proffering milk, wiping tears: by the time it returns from its aside, the voice, she's unconscious beneath the sheets, one hand entangled in her hair, the other idle between her legs where the wound of birth is still healing. She's dreaming....

But no. Such dreams this voice can't conjure.

And there've been other, more dire lapses of narrative attention. Another character, a man later to have befriended and guided our young mom, given her the means to grasp her predicament (in terms of the Tarot, the Hermit reversed: *the absurdity of birth, of singleness, separation...*), was in fact completely misplaced by the voice on a late-night train trip between Montpellier and Nice in the south of France. During an unnecessarily long-winded digression concerning modern French philosophy—concerning, to be more specific, Gilles Deleuze's use of Duns Scotus's concept of *haecceity*, that is *thisness*, or *hereness and nowness*, a mode of becoming-self neither as object, nor as subject, but as event, as assemblage, a selfhood like that, for instance, of an autumn evening—during this digression, as I say, our man simply got off the train (at Arles? Marseille? Toulon? Cannes? *no way to know*) dissolving as it were into the unseasonal blizzard, the snow-fogged mediterranean night. Nor has he cropped up since.

Buk, was his name—he insisted on the *outré* spelling. He's these days, needless to say, the envy of all our other characters.

The Kingdom of Heaven 34

H u m

The question posed by this text, as indeed by any text, is the question *why this text*? Why these words, why precisely this set of words? Why not a radically different set of words, or for that matter why not a *slightly* different set of words? If he'd sat down at the desk the day before, for instance, or the day after, in different weather, in a different mood, in a different pair of slippers, one at least of the poem's thirty-two words would surely have been different. No? He'd have given us a different Glenn Gould, would he not? Just as Glenn Gould gave us, on different days, different *Goldbergs*, for instance—albeit always distinctly Gouldesque, distinctly Gouldish *Goldbergs*—gave us in effect *Goldberg* variations, variations on the *Variations*. We would have been given a different Gould, just as Gould gave us, on different days, different Bachs—all of them distinctly Gouldesque, of course, distinctly Gouldish—different Beethovens, different Schoenbergs. We'd be in possession now of a different poem. That day, after all, the day on which he composed the poem, can hardly have been the day on which the subject of the poem first occurred to him, though it may well have been the day on which this subject first occurred to him as the subject of a poem. The poem's subject must surely have occurred to him before, but never before as a poetic subject. Why not? This subject, after all—Gould's humming—is so clearly now a poetic subject. Why was this not clear to him before, why did it become clear to him on that day and on no other? In other words, *why this poem*? This is as always the primary question posed by the poem, alongside the secondary question, why was Gould humming? Why was he always humming? Why, as he performed his peculiar, his pellucid magic on that piano (a modified Steinway, CD318), as he produced his peculiar, pellucid Bachs, his peculiar, pellucid Beethovens, his peculiar, pellucid Schoenbergs, did he have to hum along? Why, in the process of making manifest the elements of these *structures*, the intricacy of these *structures*, did he have to hum along? Why did he have to do it *out loud*, for pity's sake, so that the rest of us had no choice but to listen? Why this incessant *muttering* along with the music? Because his mother—his first and most rigorous teacher, after all—made him do it, perhaps? Because that piano, that most Gouldesque, most Gouldish of pianos—which was after all still *only a piano*—refused to perform perfectly, because those fingers, those most Gouldesque, most Gouldish of fingers—which were after all still *only fingers*—refused to perform perfectly? Because it helped Gould to *leave*, perhaps, this humming, to become absent, to withdraw yet further into the impeccable soundbox of his skull? Or on the contrary, because it helped him to *arrive*, to impress upon us his presence as one who was wilfully *choosing to be absent*?...

In no way does the poem answer these questions. It does however raise them, along with the even more central question, *why this poem*? Why these thirty-two little syllables about Glenn Gould (a Japanese tanka, incidentally, 5-7-5-7-7 syllables plus the title, *Hum*)? Why this Glenn Gould and not another? Hm?

Snow

The great ones, he says, are those who fall silent.
Hm, she says.
The great ones, he says, are those who speak, who compose, then fall silent. Look at Walser, he says, look at Sibelius. The Swiss, the Finn. Dreamers. Fabulists. Men who demanded so much of themselves that they had no choice in the end but to fall silent. Men so self-effacing as to barely exist, so self-conscious as to evaporate.
Hm, she says.
Men who died, he says, both of them, the year I was born, interestingly enough. Not that I'm trying to make any big deal out of that.
Hm, she says.
Men who fell silent and stayed that way, stayed silent for the last third of their lives, he says. From about the time my parents were born, interestingly enough.
Hm, she says.
Walser insane, Sibelius serene, equally silent, he says. Walkers, he says, men like me, men walking in order to get away, to disappear. To destroy themselves. Men moving, losing themselves in motion. Northern men, nature lovers. Great men appalled by greatness, he says, rejecting greatness, walking alone and silent through the silently falling snow. Powerful men refusing power. Constantly in the process of erasing themselves, he says, first through art, next through silence, he says. Through sound, first of all, and then through silence, through snow, he says.
Hm, she says.
Men alone in a snowy landscape, he says, seeking to leave, to leave the landscape alone. Men seeking to clarify themselves, to become so perfectly clear that we can't fail to see through them, to see the landscape they've seen. Men constantly corroding themselves with self-criticism.
Hm, she says.
Men happy, he says, happy men in a constant state of horror. I'm such a fucking moron.
Darling, she says.
I mean it. But I mean, maybe the greatest men of all are those who never say a thing, he says, who hold their peace, who fall silent before they've spoken. Men like me, he says.
Hm, she says.

The Living

If the poem had not been written, the poem would not be tolerable. The existence of the poem, if it had not been brought into existence, if it had not been born, would not be tolerable. Only the birth of the poem redeems the dead thing which is the poem. The poem, which concerns itself almost solely with death, with the death of things, and is itself of course a dead thing, was at one moment born, a birth which precisely redeems it. These words too, of course, these words on the topic of the birth and death of the poem, these words are dead, full of death as you read them, yet they're at this moment being born....

I'm dead, reads the poem, words tolerable to us only because they've been written by the living.

Triptyque: *Imagining Mallarmé*

I: *Un Blasphème*

Come to this story as a thief. Steal it. Steel yourself to imagine.... Imagine the man who in Paris, 1920, snatched a satchel at the *Gare St. Lazare* (that great iron-work station, sibilant with mist and steam —perhaps you know it from Monet), fled with it to his rented room just off nearby *place de l'Europe* (across the *pont de l'Europe*, from which Stéphane Mallarmé so routinely contemplated a final vault into the void). Imagine this man, this thief, alone, anglophone—he was never caught, so imagine him as you please. *No one will ever know.* Imagine him, say, a commercial traveller, a first-time crook. He steals not out of greed, but out of some deeper despair, a desperate need to act, to take action in the face of his isolation. Imagine his long slender fingers, how they tremble as they draw closed the lace curtains, unhook the satchel's clasp. Imagine their gentleness as they tease the satchel open, ease a rumpled manuscript out onto the rumpled bed. Its top page blank: an explicit absence. A virginity. Imagine our criminal's quickening pulse. Quivering, he turns the page. Poetry, it appears, hand-written. No name: you, only you are in a position to know that these are Roger Fry's preliminary translations of Mallarmé—of poems composed a few blocks away, in a tiny, child-infested flat in the *rue de Rome*—that no other copy of the work exists. It must strike this man as miraculous, mind you, that these are words in his own tongue, though their arrangement on the page is deeply strange:

> *A lace curtain stands effaced*
> *In doubt of the supreme Game*
> *Unfolding like a blasphemy*
> *On eternal bedlessness....*

Again, absence. A presence shot through with absence. Sweet suction from the void....

Imagine the man who's taken these lines, how he's overwhelmed, taken by them. Removed. Stolen away....

Steal away.

II: *Le Soleil*

What to compare it to, this search for an image? What image for this need to imagine?... Imagine Mallarmé in search of an image for his own search, his own striving after purity, his longing savagely to be released, sanctified. His desire to be martyred to his own task, martyred to beauty and to nothingness, to the conjuring of beauty from nothingness. Imagine him imagining: *what are you doing?* An image is forming in his head, Mallarmé's head, the image of Saint John's head released from Saint John's body, severed by the winglike scythe. *What is he doing?* The head soars, cooling as it traces its gaze upwards into the azure. It's the feast of Saint John, today, the summer solstice. The golden disk of the sun pauses overhead, over Mallarmé's head, as Saint John's head pauses in his head at its apogee, the exhaustion of its ascent. Sentient though separate from life, emancipated from the body's dissent. The head speaks, cries out in the climax of death: the poem is slashed free of the poet's body. It rises until it can rise no further, and then it falls....

Imagine the poem as a rise, and then a fall. *What are you doing?* Imagine Salome (as in Moreau) confronted by the haloed head hovering over her on its golden dish, haunted by her failure to desire. Hold the thought of her, the thought of her transfixed, body frozen by the saint's pure vision....

Let her go.

III: *L'éternité*

You have before you a photograph, black and white, of a middle-aged Mallarmé. This should help. He stands stiffly, darkly suited, in his suite of rooms in the *rue de Rome*. His glance angles upwards, over your head. Behind him on the wall he sits (in Manet's portrait), part raven, part faun, eyes falling, hand resting on an open *cahier* the contents of which you can only imagine.... Imagine yourself at one of his *Mardis*, Mallarmé's *Mardis*, one of his Tuesday gatherings. Manet's there, Redon, Verlaine, the rest, crammed into the smoke-filled flat. You sit: Mallarmé stands. "To be truly a man," he has said, "to be nature capable of thought, one must think with one's entire body...." One must resist decapitation. He waits silently, now, Mallarmé—this is your chance. Ask him. *Is this the Work, the Book? Are these notes for the grand Orphic explanation of the Earth, your opus, your torture and joy?* Look him in the face (which you may know also from Gauguin, from Renoir), say, *Is this the work through which you've sought to efface yourself, to become at last perfectly impersonal, occupied by the emptiness of things? Will it ever end? Will it begin? Or is it, by its nature as pure presence, destined eternally to be postponed?...*

And now the answer. You'll provide it yourself. Mallarmé, after all, is absent, has always been absent. You're there with him in imagination; in imagination he's elsewhere. To be the author of a work of which there's no author is surely to have learned not to be there at all, to be transformed by eternity (as he once said of the dead Poe, the poet he'd translate) into a self which is the site of the constant annihilation of self. It's to have learned to be gone—a trick picked up, perhaps, from the angel of his fallen son. Imagine that. Imagine Mallarmé standing there before you, gone....

Go with him.

Prayer

for S.

You'd love to put her in a poem, this most poetic of creatures, after all, this miracle of softness and earth-scent that sleeps beside you, miraculously, each night. But you suspect you never will. It's not so much that nothing rhymes with her—there's handy, of course, dandy, and (this would do) randy—but that her very nearness forbids it. She's too much a part of you, of the self you seek to escape. She's your happiness, not your redemption—nor are you hers. The motion is away, always away, leaving this trite, this hackneyed version of yourself behind. You're bursting, stealing out into space, like sun's light in search of what's other than itself, striving to illuminate, to become illumination. Not to show *her*, but to *show* her, bring shards of this shattered world back—bits of broken glass from the beach, sculpted by the sea—and deliver them into her hands.

What's more, you're no poet, never were. Even your praise, even your prayer is prosaic: let her drink her fill of life, and life of her.

Experience

I'm writing in application for the position advertised by your firm in this week's *Standard*. Enclosed please find my C.V., which outlines my employment history relevant to the job. In this covering letter I'll detail my academic studies, which I believe especially qualify me to join your staff.

My undergraduate degree (Honours) was interdisciplinary: my major was mathematics, but included considerable course work in literature and anthropology. At the masters level I concentrated on literary criticism and philosophy, with a post-structuralist bent. My thesis concerned the modern quest for the limit experience, the project of re-inventing the self at a sexual level—that is, of deconstructing the traditional, genital-valorized sexual body and reconstructing it as pure innovation, pure self-creation. I connected this to the feminist project of undermining the binary, dominant/submissive structure of socialized eroticism.

At the doctoral level, my work aimed at a synthesis of the mathematical and literary/philosophical strains in my studies. My point of departure was the following sentence from Søren Kierkegaard: "For the poet purchases the power of words, the power of uttering the dread secrets of others, at the price of a little secret he is unable to utter...." I connected this notion of incompleteness in literary systems to the inherent incompleteness of mathematical systems established by Kurt Gödel, suggesting that the poet, like the mathematician, gains consistency only at the cost of producing sentences which are undecidable within her oeuvre. I would, of course, gladly forward you a copy of my dissertation should you wish to include it in your assessment.

There are a number of ways in which I believe this academic experience prepares me for the position of receptionist with your firm. First of all, my grounding in a wide variety of disciplines equips me to deal effectively with people from all walks of life. Studies in anthropology have given me insights into the workings of various demographic sub-groups, while immersion in literature has nurtured my powers of empathy. An extensive analysis of Gödel's incompleteness theorem has made me comfortable with the openness and uncertainty which are so much a part of office life. My word-processing skills have been finely honed by the several drafts of my three hundred and fifty page dissertation. Finally, the time pressures attendant upon academic pursuits—for which funding is always in danger of drying up—have accustomed me to working quickly under pressure.

Please accept this as a serious application for the position of receptionist in your packaging division. I am available for work immediately.

Thanks for your attention.

Yours sincerely,

Field Trip

Twenty-five years now you've been bringing them out here, your students, your little Melanies and Michaels and Mohammeds, in their little rain jackets and their red rubber boots, to line them up at the river's edge and show them life, show them death. *No shouting. No sudden movements. No throwing things in the water. The fish are easily disturbed and if we disturb them they won't spawn, and if they don't spawn there won't be any little fish to swim downstream to the sea, and if there aren't any little fish to swim downstream to the sea there won't be any big fish to swim back upstream and spawn, and we wouldn't want that now would we, class?* You're a little late this year, to tell the truth, the peak of the season has passed and there are more dead salmon than there are live salmon to fight and fuck, one of the little boys actually said that one year, *fight and fuck*, you nearly fainted but of course he was right, that's what you bring them here to see, the male fish actually growing great hooked jaws and teeth to tear into each other for the privilege of emptying their milch out over the cloud of eggs emitted by the female, ten seconds of relief before bellying up. No contact—a sort of parallel dance. Mutual masturbation you might call it, dear God you'd better watch yourself. *No, don't touch the dead fish, don't touch anything here, it all matters.* Life reduced to matter. Dead fish strewn like driftwood along the bank, beneath ancient cedars in their pelts of moss, dead fish draped over rocks out in the river, flesh faded yellow and grey, eyes devoured already by the greedy gulls turned connoisseur in the midst of this plenty. Salmon dying as they mate, mating as they die. Sex and death. Matthew, your husband, rolling off you dead one night a decade ago, dear God don't think of it. Don't think of it. Sex and death not opposites at all, as it turns out, but parallel means of passing yourself on: reproduce and rot. Two techniques for handing down the order that is your organism. But of course Matthew hadn't wanted them, hadn't wanted children, and you wanted Matthew. Perhaps he knew. Perhaps he saw that he wouldn't live, that his children would mourn him before they knew him. Don't think of it. And teaching, a third technique. *Each female produces thousands of eggs, class, listen now, from which two offspring must reach maturity to complete the cycle.* As you've tutored thousands of children, two of whom may remember you and what you taught. As I remember you, remember the words that twenty-five years ago streamed from your beautiful young mouth. Teach, as you taught me, and then rot. Let the world hear you, and then eat you. Feed us.

Piece

The paint, when she pops back the lid, is insanely blue, perfect and potent as this moment. She bends forward, bows. She licks the liquid as though she were licking the sky and it liked it. As though the sky were coming in her mouth.

This is joy that burns her tongue. With this tongue of joy she begins her declaration. Her tongue moves over the cracked and knotted plywood like some ancient slow beast in one of her nightmares. After each letter she reloads it with paint, licks out a little more of her message. When she's done she steps back, sky dripping down her chin like blood down the chin of a vampire.

Go Too Far

She smiles. She hears cars slowing behind her, senses a crowd beginning to gather. She turns. She sees horror on these faces, she sees disgust, rage. This isn't enough.
Nothing's enough.
She goes further.

News

Watching the news this evening, in the front room with his mug of decaf and his plate of ginger snaps, Ben gets to wondering, as is his habit at this time of day. These refugees, for instance, currently flooding (refugees, he's noticed over years of news-viewing, have a tendency to "pour" or to "flood", even on occasion to "flock") these Rwandan refugees currently flooding over the border into Zaire (or is it Zambia?): could there actually be a million of them now in one frontier village, as the newscaster is claiming? How can it be called a village in the first place, if it has room enough in it for a million people? A million worlds, really, a million universes.

A similar thought had first come to Ben some years ago, at a time when Billie, his wife, was still alive, when they were still happily sharing this little retirement suite, the two of them. Two worlds, really, two universes. He'd asked himself then: how can two universes have been compressed into this one suite, as they clearly have been? For no matter how long they stuck together, he and Billie—forty-eight years, in the end—no matter how close they grew, their worlds were still irredeemably and absolutely separate. As proof of this, Ben thinks, doesn't his world exist to this very day? Isn't he currently living in it? Billie, too, lives on in Ben's world—albeit as a dead woman—but where is Billie's world now, that Ben could ever get back inside it? Didn't Billie's world in truth simply collapse, like a punctured balloon, at the moment Billie's breath ran out?

Ben sighs heavily, sips at his coffee. On the screen refugees are still to be seen staggering about, skeletal, empty-eyed, bandaged, many with bundles on their heads: the expression "worldly possessions" pops into Ben's mind just before the newscaster—an attractive oriental woman for whom Ben has a warm, almost a gushy feeling—pops it into a sentence. These people, a million or so of them (such estimates often turn out to be high, Ben's noticed, settling in his own mind on a more realistic figure of eight hundred and fifty thousand), these people are a part of Ben's world now, though he rather suspects he's not a part of theirs. These eight hundred and fifty thousand worlds must have much in common, he considers, a certain set of so-called objects, for instance, a set of motifs which must bear at least a family resemblance to one another. Yet each perfectly discrete, perfectly unique. They penetrate one another's worlds, in other words, these people, yet their worlds fail to interpenetrate.

Ben finds this thought pleasing in its symmetry, its subtlety; he nibbles at a ginger snap, not registering any longer the melee on the screen. He sits contentedly thinking his thought, and at the same time another thought, which is that there is yet another thought which he's choosing just now not to think, and that he must continue to make this choice, not to think this thought, for the rest of his life, and that he must never under any circumstances permit himself even to wonder what this thought might be.

Park Bench

My first thought, my first new thought was that everything's strange. I woke up, and without even opening my eyes I was able to reach the conclusion that everything's strange.

To have been asleep, surely, is strange, I thought to myself, to have been here and yet not to have been here, and then to wake up, to arrive at a place I already occupy, this surely is strange. Or even stranger.

At this point a refinement occurred to me: that there are two forms of the strange, the *strange* and the *radically strange*. To have been asleep is strange, for instance, I thought to myself, but then to wake up is radically strange. That space is full of objects is strange, certainly, but that objects are full of space is radically strange. I became aware, at this moment, of the edges of the boards of the park bench pressing into my back, and of the odd angle at which my head was tilted so that the knobby protuberance at the back of my skull—occiput, is it?—so that my occiput settled down comfortably between two slats. To be inside a body, to be inside this structure of sensations is strange, I thought to myself, but to have this body inside of me is radically strange. So far so good.

I opened my eyes. The strangeness of everything in sight was immediately apparent. I raised my head slightly. The fact that I did this, that I raised my head slightly, was strange, but the fact that I did anything, anything at all, was radically strange. Surely, though, there must exist ambiguous, even unresolvable cases. The notion that everything's either strange or radically strange, for instance: is this notion strange or radically strange? No clear verdict presented itself to me.

I felt unnerved, unsettled.

An elderly gentleman carrying a plastic bag sat down on the bench next to mine. He drew a bottle of vodka out of the bag, set the bottle on the bench beside him, blew his nose on the bag, folded it and tucked it into his jacket pocket as though it were a fine linen handkerchief. The prospect that we were connected, this man and I, that we were essentially one and the same was clearly strange, but the prospect that we were separate, absolutely and unalterably separate struck me as radically strange.

This instance came as confirmation, and somewhat comforted me.

I closed my eyes, eased my head back into its notch, and blacked out again.

Out

And when was our last b.m.?
Our last b.m.?
I'm sorry, sir, when was *your* last b.m.?
One o'clock.
Was that a.m. or p.m.?
P.m.
Mm-hmm. Firm or loose?
Jesus. It was loose.
A little loose, would you say, or very loose?
For God's sake. Nurse, it was very loose. It was incredibly loose. In fact, in fact, I'm glad you asked me about this, nurse, I'm relieved you brought it up. The truth is, it was *monumentally* loose. It was—
Sir, there's no need to get excited. This is routine.
I can't help it. I'm sorry, nurse. Talking about b.m.'s gets to me, it just does. It reminds me—do know what it reminds me of, nurse, talking about b.m.'s? It reminds me of my little girl. When she was just tiny, my Melissa, this is thirty years ago now—
Sir, the other patients are trying to sleep.
So was I, nurse, until just now. Let me finish. Thirty years ago. She wasn't taking much in, Melissa, I don't know what it was. Anyway, the doctor told us to keep track of her b.m.'s, tally up what came *out* so we could estimate what had gone *in*, do you see. We were to make note of each event, what time, what consistency, how much. You didn't ask me that, by the way, nurse. You didn't ask me how much.
My little boy was the same.
Pardon?
My little boy. Didn't latch on very well, so we kept a chart of his movements. We'd get so excited when he had one, and we'd put it down, you know, *large b.m., loose, yellow, two a.m.*, or whatever.
You have a little boy?
Yes.
How old?
Six, now.
Jesus. What's his name?
Patrick.
Patrick. And how are his b.m.'s these days?
His b.m.'s are very good, sir. Thank you.
Arthur. My name's Arthur.

Of course. Arthur. Just for the record, Arthur, how much?
Not much, I'm afraid. Not much at all.

Preface

We lifted the title for this anthology of scentual writings, writings on the sense of smell—*On All Fours*—from a line in "Panties", Nathan Rosenbaum's erotic tale of an anosmatic (a man with a bum nose) and his redemption, his recovery of the power of olfaction in the proximity of a new lover. This is the kind of sensual rebirth we're striving to enact in this volume. The phrase *On All Fours* evokes for us the combined sense of animality and devotion after which we went sniffing with our collective editorial nose.

The sense of smell has been denigrated in us humans, attenuated, repressed. Ever since we first reared up on our hind legs we've sought to valorize the distant, abstract, apollonian senses of sight and hearing, to spurn the proximal senses, particularly the chemical senses of taste and smell, just as we've sought in general to privilege information over sensation. Scent moves, disturbs, delights us: it forces us to feel, to remember, rather than to ratiocinate. The repression of scentual knowledge—which since long before Freud has been linked to the rise of civilization—is a denial of the body, of instinct, of nature. It's a denial of mother earth, and beyond that, of femaleness itself, whose fecund emanations we've for so long sought to sterilize. To repress our olfactory powers is to repress passion, recollection—recall the Proustian moment, at which scent unlocks the lost self encoded in memory—and most deeply perhaps to repress our awareness of evanescence. Scents waft past us and away: to admit them is to admit that all things pass.

Scent, in other words, is a destabilizing sense. A subversive sense. A twitching nostril is as revolutionary a sign as a scrawl of graffiti. It's in this sense that our anthology is meant to be seditious. The very act of writing about scent, we believe, undermines the orthodox opposition of body and culture. It employs the tools of culture to root around in the pungent soils of our personal and collective experience, a deeply sexual process——as a pig's rooting for truffles can be construed as sexual, motivated as it is by the piggish pheromones those fungi emit. To write about scent is to invite the reader back down to earth, back down on all fours—the dionysian stance—the better to smell the soil, to smell each other, the better to mate, to pray.

Following the stereochemical scheme of John E. Amoore, we've divided this volume into seven sections, along the lines of his seven primary odours: Camphoraceous, Musky, Floral, Pepperminty, Ethereal, Pungent, Putrid. A scratch-and-sniff at the beginning of each section will give readers a concrete sense of what's intended by these definitions; from the volume as a whole, when each of these odours has been released, should arise a pure, conglomerate scent, an absolute emanation, just as white light arises from the confluence of all the colours.

Spree

There are two questions, she thinks to herself, the question of poverty and the question of the nature of poverty. *Josh, push gently, honey.* The question of poverty, she thinks to herself, often amounts to the question of quality versus quantity. *Don't kick, Sandra, or you'll have to get out and walk.* One slice of whole grain bread, for instance, costs the same as two slices of white bread. *No.* The question of poverty in this case, then, is the question of whether it's easier to think with empty blood or empty belly. *No.* But the question of the nature of poverty is a different question altogether, she thinks to herself. *Maybe next time.* The question of the nature of poverty raises the question of whether it's wise to think at all. *Josh, honey, let the lady past.* Because to think is to desire, at the very least to desire to think, yet to be in perfect poverty is to refrain from all desiring. *No, I'm afraid not.* The mystics say we must be poor even in will. *Not so hard.* They want us to know as little and want as little as when we weren't. *A kangaroo?* We must be nothing. *Just a lucky guess.* These are the thoughts of people who haven't had much to eat. *Put that back, honey.* In this sense, what's always beyond me is poverty. *No.* No matter how little I have I haven't poverty. *You know why, sweetness.* To be truly in poverty is to be emptied out infinitely, to be dispossessed of oneself, of the possibility of oneself. *I'm sorry.* To be in poverty is to be without even a void in oneself begging to be filled. *I'm sorry.* Without even a prayer. *No, and this is the last time I'm telling you.* To be in poverty is to be free of everything, simply to be. *Nothing.*

The Kingdom of Heaven 54

Untitled LXIX

[While I'm in general loathe to offer commentary on my own poetic offerings, which ought after all to be independent creations, creatures capable of making their own way in the world, there are difficulties presented by this particular piece, both technical and thematic, which incline me to preface it with a few remarks.

It's my perspective here that sexuality is fundamentally oral —that is, that all sex acts are acts of cannibalism, or, ideally, sublimated cannibalism. Sexuality is in this sense the metaphorical resolution of the dualism of self and other, eater and eaten. Through the equations penis-breast, vagina-mouth, we come to view the coital couple as a pair of infants latched on to one another, ingesting one another, incorporating one another, simultaneously meeting their two conflicting needs: to consume the universe, to be consumed by the universe. To eat and be eaten, to become and to disappear. Lovers are in other words one another's host, and copulation eucharistic.

This is the conceptual framework of the piece. As far as technical aspects are concerned, I believe it's sufficient to observe that the goal of poetics is always to match form to content, and that the stylistic departure here (from my more accustomed forms of sonnet and ballade) is justified by my chosen subject matter. B.B.]

There once was a bloke from Brighton,
Who had a taste for the ladies of the night, 'n'
   He'd serve up his Thomas,
   With a lick, and a promise
That this time he wouldn't be bitin'.

The Kingdom of Heaven

Synonyms

"Dink," says Molly. "Pecker. Penis. Prick. Cock. Wang."

"Sounds like a law firm," says Kath. "Prick, Cock, and Wang."

"Wang, Pecker, and Wang," says Molly. She draws on her cigarette, sends a great prong of smoke rearing into the air. "They always repeat one."

"Prong," says Jill. "We forgot prong."

"But they're not the same," says Molly. "Are they. A prong isn't a weeny."

"Weeny," says Kath. She giggles. She rolls towards Molly in bed, relieves her of her cigarette. "I don't smoke, either," she says. She takes a puff, closes her eyes in order to concentrate, in order not to cough. She opens them, exhales carefully, allowing the smoke to creep fog-like across the moors of Molly's chest.

"And a boob," says Molly, "isn't a breast."

They're wives, Molly and Kath. Molly's my wife, Kath's my best friend Keith's wife. This is the first time for both of them, for both women, first time with a woman's body that isn't at the same time their own body, or so I imagine, as I imagine all of this, lying in bed beside the silently sleeping Molly. She's kicked off the sheets: her body's stretched out next to mine, lit by streaks of pale blue light pouring in from the street. Still life.

"Pussy," murmurs Molly.

"Cunt," murmurs Kath.

And this is pretty much how they spend the rest of the night, searching for the perfect word, the perfect conformation of lip and tongue to name the miracle of themselves.

Watching Her Go

We're at the Blue Parrot Cafe. We've ordered a lunch special each, burger-chips-coffee-pie, from Rose, the owner's daughter. Arny's smoking again, telling me about his woman's new woman.

"She astral travels," he says. "She remembers three past lives. She was a pirate, she was one of Michelangelo's bum-boys. She was a Sumerian princess." He pauses. "Where the hell's Sumeria, Jim?"

"Africa?" I say. "Middle East. Babylon, and all that."

"Right," says Arny. "And she has all this money, but she gets it *correctly*, somehow. Nothing soul-destroying, nothing earth-raping. Not for our Guinevere, no."

"Guinevere?" I say.

"She switched it from Ginny."

"Jesus," I say.

Rose comes over with our coffee.

"And she has an orgasm a night," says Arny. "Thanks. Or two, three. She gets up at four-thirty in the morning to meditate." He shakes his head. "I'm lucky to hit the fucking bowl at four-thirty in the morning."

"Wait a minute," I say. "Hang on a minute. Jess *tells* you all this? I mean, she actually *tells* you all this?"

"She wants us to be open and honest with one another," says Arny. "So do I, really. I've just gotta figure out something to be open and honest about."

"Hang a crystal from your tool pouch," I say. "Join Amnesty. Join the men's movement. No, hang on, that's bad."

"I've got it," says Arny. "I'll tell her you and I are, you know, getting it on."

I look up at him. I look into his blue, his incredibly pale blue eyes. He looks into mine. We both give a huge snort of laughter.

Arny butts out his cigarette, chuckling. "Anyway, I'll think of something," he says. "I'm seeing Jess tonight. I'm taking her out for Tibetan, that should count for something. Guinevere's at rain-making class."

"Rain-making?" I say. "She takes *rain-making*?"

"Yeah," says Arny. He's quiet a moment. "You know, it may be true," he says. "An awful lot of things are true."

"Uh-huh," I say.

Rose comes over with our burgers. She bends over the table, concentrating, as she sets them down. Arny and I watch. I know he's as fascinated as I am by the way her body shifts under her stiff white blouse, by the contrast.

"Thanks," I say.

"Thanks," says Arny.

Rose nods, turns to walk away.

Arny and I sit there, watching her go.

Desert

    She was meant to marry the dockworker, originally, the *stevedore*—I'd always wanted to use that word—for political reasons, namely to piss off her upper-middle-class parents, and after lots of gymnastic sex bear a young boy named Anatole, who'd be deaf, or blind, or both. That was my idea, that's how the story was shaping up. There was an awful lot of symbolism involved. An incredible amount, really. At the class level, but also psychologically, spiritually. I had the opening roughed in, characters introduced and so on, all except Anatole, when I quit for a snack. I clicked on the tube, what the hell. There was this woman on the screen, a black woman out in a desert somewhere. Flies crawled in and out of her nostrils. Skin clung to her skeleton, her belly ballooned out. With hunger, I assumed. Suddenly, though, she squatted down, shut her eyes, and had a baby. Right there on the screen, just squeezed it out, all violet and slick. A child. What the hell was I supposed to do?

    I went back to work. Trouble was, things had changed. My heroine stopped eating. She just stopped. Her stevedore reasoned with her as best he could, her parents sent her to the most expensive man in town. No use. Her flesh burned away, her eyes grew huge and brilliant, her breasts collapsed. Anatole was just a fond whimsy of the stevedore's now, a dream with nowhere to roost.

    I still don't know where it'll end. It doesn't worry me. What worries me is that I might just as easily have turned to any other channel. I might have turned to the tennis match, or to the talk show on telepathic midgets who love too much. There was no reason for me to turn to that desert scene that had anything to do with the story itself. Certain things have happened to me, others haven't. A shape has gradually emerged from it all, but I have to ask myself, could this be me? Could this be me?

Kevin

"Kevin," I said, because this was my name, or rather, this was the moment at which it became my name. We'd all been there, the whole class, but only one of us had actually pulled the alarm because only one of us *could* pull the alarm, of course, it was only possible for one of us to pull the alarm, at which moment it occurred to the rest of us that we were all innocent now that only one of us was guilty. At the moment one of us became guilty the rest of us became innocent, or rather, at the moment the rest of us became innocent one of us became guilty, a little brown-haired, big-eared boy named Peter, who had in fact curled his fingers around the handle of the alarm and pulled it down. At that moment, as the bell began to sound, it occurred to the rest of us that none of the rest of us had pulled it down because only one of us had pulled it down, and it occurred to Peter that this was occurring to us, and he turned pale, terribly pale, and started to cry, and bolted off down the hall. And when the Principal, the grey-haired, great-nostrilled Principal arrived and the alarm had finally been silenced we were all still very clear about this, that none of us were guilty, so that when he began to collect names we offered them up, our names, as though this were the most innocent thing in the world to do. "Kevin," I said, when my turn came, and at this moment I became conscious of the fact that the Principal was gathering a list of names that would not include the name Peter, that as each of us said our name, Sandra or Kate or Kevin, we were in fact saying the name Peter, the name of the only one of us who had fled. "Kevin," I said, and at this moment I became conscious of myself, conscious of the fact that I was guilty of having failed to be conscious of myself, conscious of the fact that in saying the name Kevin I was in fact saying the name Peter. "Kevin," I said, and became conscious of myself. Kevin.

Third World

It's only my breasts, she thinks. *In all other respects I'm perfect, perfectly first world*, she thinks. *My hands, for instance, look at my hands*, holding them up over her head, fingers splayed. Slender and pale and soft, long hard pink nails. *And my spandex-ready thighs*, she thinks. *And my eyes*, she thinks, *my eyes*, closing them in order to see them, to gaze into them. *Pale blue and piercing*, she thinks. She sits up in bed, glancing down as her breasts fall away from her rib cage, down and away. *Not melons, these breasts, but sweet potatoes*, she thinks. *Not Vogue so much as National Geographic.*

The door of the bathroom opens and a man walks into the bedroom. The same man she'd brought up with her the night before, presumably, to this hotel room, though she scarcely recognizes him now. A small, brown, almost hairless man. He stands in the doorway, looking sheepish, bemused. Perhaps he's hung over. His penis dangles between his legs, pendulous, its head averted slightly in a gesture of modesty, or coquetry.

"Come," she says, dramatically, spreading her arms.

The man moves, hesitantly enough, across the room and around to her side of the bed. As he kneels, she takes his head between her hands and guides it, almost forces it, to her breast, directing his lips to her nipple.

"There, there," she murmurs. "Take your time. There's enough for all of you."

Speak

Two rooms.

In the first, a dentist's office—bright, sunlit, postered with puppies and butterflied glades—a man reclines in the patient position. His wide-open mouth bristles with instruments; he experiences only an intermittent pressure at the back of his jaw, a tingling in his fat tongue. He attempts to speak, to banter with the dentist, but fails to make himself understood. He chuckles. His nostrils twitch at the scent of powdered tooth. Painless but unpleasant, this experience: he endeavours to transport himself elsewhere, to fathom someone less fortunate than himself. He imagines a man in another room, a similar room, undergoing a similar treatment, but with certain differences. No anaesthetic, for instance, a less benign hand....

In the second room, a parody of the first—at a distance of some tens or hundreds or thousands of miles from it—another man reclines in a dentist's chair. His body is securely shackled to the chair's steel frame, which has been stripped of all cushioning, his head immobilized by a leather band cinched tight across his brow. The room—referred to as The Office by the government officials who bring their prisoners here—is essentially a concrete bunker: dank, windowless, brilliant with cold fluorescent light. Two Assistants loiter at the door, chewing on toothpicks. The Dentist hovers over his Patient, drill in hand.

"Spit it out," the Dentist murmurs. "Speak. Just one more name, is all we need. Then you can go home, you'd like that, wouldn't you? No more Appointments...."

The Dentist has been making this offer, or an offer very like it, every few minutes throughout the previous eight Appointments, each of which has been four hours in duration (eternity, as it turns out, is half the length of a working day).

If he had any names available to him, of course, the Patient would spit them out instantly, along with the blood and tooth that threaten to choke him. But he has none. He hasn't his own name, or the name of any other person or thing: these names are gone, language itself is gone, sucked out of him by his torturer and turned into something dark and delectable that makes him chuckle as he works. The Patient has only moans to offer up now, whimpers, screams. Half an hour or so ago a word materialized in his mind, miraculously—the word "puppy". He howled it out, without hesitation, through ruined mouth, as though it were an incantation that had the power to set him free.

"Good for you!" the Dentist had congratulated him, setting his drill aside briefly to jot the word in his notebook. One more piece of vital information....

"Well, that should do it," says the dentist. "No chewing on that side for the rest of the day, right?"

The patient nods, rising from the chair. He feels groggy, shaken, as though returning from some dark dream. He moves his jaw gingerly, experimentally. He prepares to speak.

Damage

I'd been reading, or rather I'd been re-reading a novel by the Dutch author Harry Mulisch about an incident in German-occupied Holland during the war, about, in a more general way, *damage*, or rather the *denial of damage*. Inside the book's cover I discovered a biographical note explaining that Mulisch had been born to a Jewish mother—whose family was wiped out in the concentration camps—and to an Austrian father who was jailed after the war for collaborating with the Nazis. Mongrel offspring of a Jew and a Nazi, Mulisch's conscience, it occurred to me, must have taken on an eery consonance with that of his age. How magnificently clear it must have been to Mulisch what his life's work would be. Reading his novel left me feeling strangely devoid of identity, devoid of voice.

The book had been given to me by an old girlfriend, a German-born woman, who'd had a mania for the literature of the Second World War. A fixation. Leni was a passionate, an angry woman: she'd made love to me angrily, lectured me angrily, and left me angrily, for another woman, a Jewish student of mine in the English department, named Rachel. In the front of the book, a paperback, across from the biographical note, Leni had written, "To Georgie, with love, from a boyish girl to a girlish boy, son of tyrant and tyrannized, androgynous son of *a man and a woman....*xox."

Why did I let Leni go so easily? I found myself wondering. Why is it that I've always felt such relief when women give up on me? I knew I'd loved her, loved Leni, loved and desired her, yet the greatest joy I'd ever received was in the act of releasing her. How could this be?

I happened to be at that point in Mulisch's book at which his protagonist, Anton—a boy orphaned under horrendous circumstances during the war—has grown up to become an anaesthesiologist. He speculates, in one haunting digression, that anaesthesia does not in truth kill pain, but only the ability to express pain, and to remember pain. "When patients woke up," Mulisch wrote, "it was always evident that they had been suffering." Yet they could remember nothing, relate nothing. They lived on oblivious to the tissue not only of pain but of solace which now underlay the structure of their lives.

Lipstick

To our readers: Lengthy editorial deliberation has preceded the publication of this short piece, which has raised for us once again issues of cultural appropriation, of authenticity of voice. Our decision in this instance has been to run the piece as submitted, complete with its own fictionalized editorial, but to make explicit the identity of the author, one Susan Hill, who we've established beyond a reasonable doubt to be an upper-middle-class lesbian childless woman of colour. With this knowledge, we believe, our readers are in a position to reach their own judgements as to the validity of this voice and its point of view. [The Editors]

Invalid

To our readers: As our regular readers will recognize, "Invalid" is being run here for a second time, a circumstance which requires some explanation on our part. At the time of its first appearance, "Invalid" was understood to have been authored by Pop Sickle, described in our Notes on Contributors as "an HIV-positive gay male marxist rap artist and author of colour." Since that time, however, it has come to our attention that this authorship was pseudonymous, not to say mischievous, that the piece was in fact written by one Brenda MacIntyre, an uninfected white working-class heterosexual single mother of three. With this change in authorship, we believe, the piece itself is altered, and so we run it again here for purposes of comparison. [The Editors]

When I woke up he was gone. I'm such a sound sleeper, especially after a passionate, an athletic night like that one. We'd taken each other every which way: picturing it all again I felt a brand new stirring beneath the sheets. I crawled out of bed, padded around the apartment in search of some sign of him, a note, a phone number. Nothing. Then, on the bathroom mirror, in lipstick (a vibrant pink, his, not mine):

Health cannot analyze itself even if it looks at itself in the glass. It is only we invalids who can know anything about ourselves.
             Italo Svevo

It's six months later, and I still can't be sure. The virus can take that long to manifest its presence in the blood. And of course, he may himself have been perfectly healthy, or damaged in some other, some noncommunicable way. He'd seemed so robust, so full of life: that's presumably why I agreed to do without precautions. But his aim was clearly to infect me in some way, at the very least with this doubt, this self-awareness which is itself a disease. A malignancy. To be ill is to know yourself, yes; to know yourself is to be ill....

We would of course appreciate the opportunity of dialoguing with members of the gay male and PWA (Persons With AIDS) communities, as well as with any representatives of the Italian literary community (Svevo himself having unfortunately passed away seventy years ago) concerning this piece. Please feel free to address your comments to the collective. [The Editors]

Yeah, like she said. [The Editors]

Dear Pitiful

I, too, at one time, suffered unbearable pathos, suffered, as you put it in your letter, "a constant and crushing tenderness, a paralysing pity for everything, for myself and all others, human and nonhuman, animal and vegetable, living and dead." I know how you feel! I set about treating myself in the common, sensible, allopathic way: I sought to *counteract* the melancholy, to neutralize it by applying its opposite, images of serenity, of ease, images of unearned and inconsequential happiness: "Curled up by the crackling fire, then, the little kitten nodded off into a deep and dreamless sleep," for instance. These treatments, while effective in the short term, ultimately failed, as all allopathic treatments must do, because they confound the organism, its natural exuberance, its longing to *express*. That's why I'm recommending to you a homeopathic treatment, that is, a treatment based on the concept of treating like with like. A homeopathic treatment employs substances which, if administered to a healthy individual, would produce the symptoms currently being experienced by the sick individual. Think of hot tea on a warm day: it warms a cool person, yet cools a warm person.

As treatment for your pathos, then, I'd prescribe an image such as the following: "A horse in a slaughterhouse, hanging suspended in midair with its throat cut, keeps galloping in the void," from Hervé Guibert's fictional treatment of the death, by AIDS, of the French thinker Michel Foucault, himself the source of a number of effective remedies. There's more pathos here—Guibert, for instance, who also turned out to be seropositive, ended up killing himself by overdosing on anti-AIDS drugs. But the key to the homeopathic cure is its minute dosage: for you I'd advise a murmuring, a barely audible recitation of the GITV (the "galloping in the void" cure, as it's known amongst practitioners) every four hours, and twice before sleep.

It's worked for me—here's hoping it works for you too!

The Tower

The days are peaceful enough, a round of chores, a routine without need of revision, but the nights get positively eery, what with the master up in his tower howling at the top of his lungs, baying at the moon you'd imagine, though most nights there is no moon. So the maids and the cooks and the gardeners and all the other staff gather in the kitchen to tell one another tales. Like this one of the doorman's:

"There once was a hunter, a lonely old man who had for company only an old dog, an old hunting dog."

"What was its name?" the butler wants to know.

"It had no name," says the doorman.

"No name? But how could that be? How could an old dog—"

"Blodwin," says the doorman. "The dog's name was Blodwin."

"Ah."

"So the hunter," the doorman continues, "had for company only an old dog named Blodwin. And one day the two of them, the hunter and his dog, were out in the fields together when they startled a goose from cover. A great fat white goose. And as it rose, this goose, the hunter hastily took aim and fired. The goose came down, but still flapping —it was only wounded."

"Where was it wounded?" the charwoman wants to know.

The doorman thinks a moment, before replying, "In the left wing, here," indicating a spot on his left arm, half way between shoulder and elbow.

"Ah."

"And Blodwin brought the goose back to the hunter and laid it at the hunter's feet," says the doorman. "And the hunter took it in his arms and carried it towards home, and as he walked the goose lay peacefully in his arms, just as though it were used to being held, and reached up with its beak to hiss softly in the hunter's ear, so softly that it sounded like whispering. And in the whispering the hunter heard all the things he hadn't heard whispered to him in so many years. And he became distracted, the hunter did, and wandered off his normal route through the woods, and before he knew it he was completely lost. And as he wandered he met an old woman coming towards him along the path, the unfamiliar path, a woman alone, who spoke to him, saying, 'Excuse me, good sir, but I am out searching for my goose, my lost goose, and can't help noticing that you are carrying such a goose in your arms. Please, she is my only companion, and speaks to me the way no one has spoken to me in so many years.' Well, you can imagine what happened after that."

"No, no we can't," say the others, their eyes imploring. For a moment there's silence, and in it, the howling.

"Okay," says the doorman, "Okay." And he goes on.

Ocean

We were just clearing away the soup bowls (our deep blue, stained with the dregs of Jenny's green gazpacho) when Jacques Cousteau walked in. Or rather waddled in, backwards: apparently that's how it's done with flippers on. Crabwise.

"Hello, Jacques." I said, "Or rather, *bonjour!*"

Jacques nodded at me—he had himself turned around by this time, and was swivelling his head, taking things in. They're like a set of blinkers, those goggles, it's a wonder how he manages.

"Ah, Monsieur Cousteau? Can I set you a place?" This from Jenny. "We've finished soup, but there's plenty of our main dish," she said. "Szechwan chicken. Larry's piece of resistance." She winked at me. "Jacques—may I call you Jacques?—do please join us."

Jacques peered about, his eyes all buggy in his blue mask. He's probably the only person I'd recognize in SCUBA gear.

I clapped my hands together, causing Jacques to startle slightly. His regulator clicked and hissed with each breath.

"Where are my manners?" I exclaimed. "Jacques, I'd like you to meet our good friends, Jill and Ted Dickson. Jill and Ted, Jacques Cousteau. Oh, and Jacques, this is my wife, Jenny, and I'm Larry. Bartly. Larry Bartly. Larry and Jenny Bartly."

I reached out to shake, but Jacques had his hands full of underwater camera gear. He shifted it all to one hand, inhaled deeply, and plucked the regulator from his mouth.

"Where is d'ocean?" he said, and popped the regulator back in.

"It's that way," we all four said in unison, pointing in the four cardinal directions: Jill east, Ted west, Jenny north, and I south.

Jacques stared at us in consternation.

"Jacques," I said, "the truth is—the truth is that there is no ocean. I—I'm sorry."

Jacques looked flabbergasted. He looked ruined. A tear formed at the corner of one of his bulgy eyes, a single salty drop, and rolled down his long nose. His goggles began to fog up.

"I know," I said, reaching out to squeeze a neoprene-enshrouded shoulder. "I know."

Despair

It's such a relief to me that she's verbal now, that she can talk. No more "Boo! Boo!"—if she wants to latch on she can say so nicely. It's what I've longed for. Someone to share my thoughts with, my ideas. A friend.

Today she comes toddling into my room. I'm gazing out the window, you know, the way adults do.

"Mommy," she says, "what are you feeling?"

I turn, smile down at her. Such a sensitive girl. I put my hand on her hair, her gorgeous golden-red hair. Just touching it brings the scent of it to me, its milky sweetness. "Despair, honey," I say. "I'm feeling despair."

She looks puzzled. "Despair?" she says.

"Or actually, I don't know *what* I'm feeling," I say. "I just know I don't know what I'm feeling. That's despair."

"But why despair, Mommy? I mean, what are you... what's...?" She sniffles, rubs her nose back and forth vigorously with the back of her hand. It creates a little crackling sound.

I laugh, lightly, the way I do. The way she loves. "Good questions, honey," I say. "It's just some little thing that's made me despair, that's made me *aware* I'm in despair. Just some little thing your Dad's gone and done. Despair's never about what made you realize you were in despair though, honey. It's about being yourself, about not being yourself. You want to be yourself, to be what you are, and yet you're not what you are, and you're nothing else. You can't escape yourself, you can't be yourself. That's despair." I stroke my daughter's cheek, pale and mottled, with the tips of my fingers.

She nods. "That cloud looks like a horsey," she says, pointing over my shoulder. She sneezes.

"Cover your mouth, honey," I say.

"Are you very often in despair, Mommy?" she says, crackling her nose again.

"Always, honey, we all are. But there's a kind of despair that isn't aware of being despair, that's so far from salvation it doesn't even long for salvation." I bend down and hoist her up in my arms. She hooks her legs over my hips, lays her head against my chest. Then she raises it again.

"Salvation?" she says.

But she's already looking away, up and away, and I decide to save all that for another time.

The Kingdom of Heaven 71

Facts Of Life

It's time my son and I had our little chat. It's been thirty years now since Dad and I had ours.

"You know where a baby comes from, don't you, boy?" Dad questioned me.

"Sure," I said. True enough: I knew a baby came from a woman's belly. I just hadn't a clue how it might make its way out.

"And you know how it gets in there in the first place?"

"Yes, *Dad*," I groaned. A friend of mine had told me all about his sister, how she'd gotten pregnant skinny-dipping in the slimy pond round back of the school.

"Good. Well, just you take precautions. Never count on a woman to protect herself. That was my mistake, and believe me, it's one you regret for the rest of your life."

So I'm determined to do better. First off, I'll let my son do the asking. That way I'll be able to gauge the level of knowledge he's ready for.

We go out for a walk one evening, just the two of us. I say to him, very casual, "You'd let me know, Son, wouldn't you, if there was anything you were wondering about the facts of life?" I put it just that way, *facts of life*.

"Well, Pop," he says to me, "There is one thing. Are...are a man's nipples considered an erogenous zone?"

"That's an excellent question, Son," I say. "But a tricky one. You see, it depends on the particular man. I can give you statistics, if that'll help. Roughly sixty percent of males demonstrate some degree of nipple tumescence, resulting in either a partial or a full erective reaction."

"Oh. And at what stage of sexual response does all this occur?"

"During plateau phase, most often. Incidentally, Son, male nipple detumescence is very slow compared to that of the female. It's the darnedest thing."

"Huh. Well, thanks, Pop. Hey, by the way, do men ever, like, lactate?"

"On occasion, Son. Given forceful and sustained suckling-like stimulation, certain men have been known to produce small quantities of milk."

We fall silent for a while. We just stroll along, father and son, enjoying the quiet summer evening. The air has cooled, but we can still feel the heat of the sun pressing up at us from the pavement. People are out on their front stoops, sipping at coffees, spooning at bowls of ice cream. It's moments like this you appreciate living in a good neighbourhood.

As we near home, my son says to me, "Pop, sometimes I wish I had breasts."

"I understand, Son," I say. "I really do." I give his shoulder a squeeze, and we traipse up the steps and in through the screen door.

For a first time, I'm thinking this went pretty well.

New Man

This time you're doing it right. This time it matters, this man *matters*. You've had a half dozen dates: flick, concert, lunch, dinner. Stroll by the sea. Tussle on the couch by the light of the tube. Time for the big step: time for him to meet your little girl.

He's waiting for you at the burger joint when you arrive. He's snagged a booth: he springs up, gives you a peck on the cheek, shakes your daughter's hand. She smiles, noncommittal.

Everybody sits. You and your daughter on one side, your new man on the other.

"Can I have a Sprite?" from your daughter. See what she can get away with here.

"No, darling. Juice or water."

"You're so *mean*," she says. She snuggles up to you, curly head on your woolly shoulder. "Hey," she says, "your hand's all hairy."

The three of you stare, together, in silence, at your new man's hand. It crouches there on the formica table-top, weirdly still, startled by the sudden glare of attention. Shyly it curls, uncurls.

"My daddy's having a vasexomy," adds your daughter, as if completing the thought. "He says enough's enough. I heard him."

"Darling—"

"I know what that *is*, Mommy," snaps your little girl, turning on you. "I'm not *stupid*."

"No darling. You're not stupid."

"Have you had a vasexomy, Mommy?" she says, and before you can respond, swivels to face your new man across the table. "Have *you* had a vasexomy?"

A longish pause. You resist the urge to rescue him, put off this moment. Sink or swim.

"No," he says at last. "No, I haven't. I *have* had the chicken pox, though."

Your little girl frowns, suspicious. "Who *hasn't*," she says. She leans forward a little. "Have you had your period?" she says.

He shakes his head, your new man. "Not yet," he says.

"Me neither," says your little girl. "Me neither."

My Dad

His idea, ironically, his passion, my dad's passion, was to immortalize himself, to make himself the centre of a story so distinctive, so potent that it would not be capable of being forgotten. The figures in this culture, he realized, who'd succeeded in this gambit, had found a place in a larger story, the central story of the culture, the story of a de-centring. The story of a removal. Copernicus, of course, removing us from the centre of the cosmos; Darwin, removing us from the centre of earthly life; Freud, removing us from the centre of ourselves. And so on. The great men, then, were those who'd forced upon us lessons in humbleness, who'd demonstrated first of all that we weren't at the centre of some particular domain, and second of all that *nothing* was at the centre of that domain, that any attempt even to define such a centre —for instance, by replacing the earth with the sun at the centre of the universe—was temporary, and in the end ludicrous.

My dad's chosen domain, of course, was story itself. His thesis was that all narrative, including the supreme narrative of our de-centring, was devoid of centre: in other words that no narrative, or narrative of narratives, was actually supreme, and that no story was about what it seemed to be about. His disappearance, then, his removal of himself from the centre of his own story was simply an extension of his life's work, a demonstration that even the story of his life wasn't about him in the first place. As, incidentally, this one isn't, either.

So you begin to see why you've never heard of my dad. And why you never will.

Possession

When it finally arrived—inspiration—I'd been sleepless two nights, pacing up and down the block in front of my house, heart palpitating with an excess of caffeine and a form of enthusiasm I call *aesthetic*, which also makes my hands quiver and a little muscle beneath my right shoulder blade—at the tip of my right wing, as it were—beat with humming-bird-like intensity. This is the solution to my creative conundrum that came to me at that time:

The woman's—Val's—dream, the dream from which she's awoken at the beginning of the first act, turns out indeed to be a dream of possession, a dream which possesses. Val comes to recognize, in the course of the second act, that what had possessed her was not in fact a man but a dream. She'd been possessed, overpowered, not by the man in her dream but by her dream of possession. The man who'd made such violent love to her in her dream, pinned her helplessly to the wall with an annihilating pleasure she'd sought to renounce, was a power greater than herself she herself had invoked, a power helpless to do anything but make love to her. She'd conjured a power with which to annihilate herself, so that she could come into and pass out of existence at the same moment, give birth to herself and crucify herself, a confluence of processes so intensely pleasurable as to allow her to come with such intensity, just as she awoke, that she almost passed out. This she'd explain to Paul in the final scene: that she needed to be possessed, but that she herself was only inadequately able to imagine the power which must possess her, that this power was perfectly *beyond her*—and thus of course beyond everybody else, including him—and that what she really needed from Paul was exactly what he needed from her, a little kindness and affection, someone to share the rent, someone to do the dishes when she cooked, and vice versa. And they'd reach out to one another, as the curtain fell, content to hold yet not to have.

This was all very well, even charming, but from my perspective it missed the point. I wasn't writing a play, after all, but a piano concerto—a composition, incidentally, which to this day remains incomplete. Yes, perhaps there were possibilities offered up of which I failed to take advantage, images of dominance and submission, wilfulness and willingness I might have translated into the lexicon of music, into this musical conversation. Still, I couldn't help but feel that a rather serious blunder had been made. It was as though I'd been briefly possessed by somebody else's daemon. I've spent a great deal of time since that day, pacing up and down the block before my house, striving to picture a playwright hunched at a desk, head in hands, in some distant part of the city, on some distant street. I drive myself nearly to distraction trying to fathom what music might have reached its climax in the hushed concert-hall of that head.

But so far, nothing.

Nothing Received

They linger over cups of espresso in an outdoor cafe on some southbank boulevard. Between them a copper ashtray bristles with spent Gitanes. Everything's pastel: blue table cloth, yellow hair, flesh-tone flesh. They're foreigners, Americans. You can tell by the boxed, clean-shaven cut of his jaw, the self-conscious elegance of her scissored legs. American papers lie wingspread on the table before them.

From his mouth curls a speech-balloon: "Says here, honey, they can suck the fat from your buttocks and belly, inject it into your boobs. Enlarge you half a cup size!"

"Says here," says her bubble, "an old woman's just been let off scotfree for beating her husband to death with a plastic bed-pan!"

I gulp white wine from my plastic cup. I shift my eyes sideways: there's a woman standing beside me, head cocked, arms akimbo, taking in the same piece. She's striking in that spiky, just-back-from-the-crypt sort of way. Black stockings and army boots. Nose ring.

"'Nothing Received'," I say, reading from the little red-stickered tag. I notice that my speech is very slightly slurred. I've been back to the refreshment table a few times: angels on horseback, fruity white wine.

She glances at me, startled, her smile unexpectedly vulnerable in light of the steel toes, the half-inch hair.

"Hey, there's nothing to be afraid of," I say.

"Yes," she says. "Yes there is."

Babe

"It's release," she says to me. She's frightened, but crystal clear. Beautiful. Perfect. Her face, her breasts. I've instructed her to take off her clothes. "It's release you're after, release from...from *this*," she says. "From being this *thing*, this single *thing*."

"I miss you, Babe," I say.

"Exactly," she says. I notice now that she's cold, that she's shivering. Clinging to herself.

"Why did you leave?" I say.

"You can't stand it, can you?" she says. "That there's difference, that anything's *different*. Don't you see? Even your hatred is love."

"Are you fucking him?" I say. "I'm going to kill him too, by the way." I remember to aim the gun at her. I've let it droop, lower its muzzle to the floor—dejected puppy.

"Please," she says.

"Fuck off," I say.

"What you really want," she says, "is to kill yourself. That's the real release, but you're frightened, frightened of missing it. You can't be released and *see* that you've been released, both. You can't be alive and dead, so you make do with sacrifice, life and death as close as you can get them. But honey, what if I watch? What if I'm your witness? You'll be released, emptied out, and I'll *see that you've been released*. I'll see you gone."

"Really?" I say. "You'd do that for me?" I can hardly believe it. And before she can speak, before she can change her mind, lose heart, I put the gun to my head and blow my brains out.

What She Asked Me

She asked me, if you had the choice, would you rather freeze to death or burn to death? Would you rather suffocate or fall off the roof?

She asked me, what's so goddam funny?

She asked me, has it really been that long? What have we been doing all this time?

She asked me, do you remember the first time we met? That party after the Pinter thing? And the bald guy who kept saying that nothing always means the same thing whether it has a big "N" or a little one? I agreed with him, but you didn't—or was it the other way around? Our first argument.

She asked me, do you mind?

She asked me, if we'd decided to have the child, what would we have called it? Andrew? Suzanne?

She asked me, is thirty-six old?

She asked me, what do you mean by God? Are you absolutely sure you mean something?

She asked me, if you were killing yourself, how do you think you'd do it? Sleeping pills? Gas? I can't see you with a gun.

She asked me, why would you be killing yourself?

She asked me, have you ever asked yourself, what if I'd gone to Africa and held starving children in my arms? What if I'd kept on?

She asked me, is the Chagall print yours or mine, I can never remember?

She asked me, what's a nine letter word for animals getting along?

She asked me, what does this mean here, "comic nihilism"?

She asked me, how much wood would a woodchuck chuck if a woodchuck could chuck wood?

She asked me, do you think it's possible to love someone, and then not to love them?

She asked me, was that asking so much?

The Kingdom of Heaven 80

Wool

The issue for her, it seems to me, comes down to whether the life she's living is *her own life* or *no one's life*. The life she's living can't possibly belong to anyone but to her, but to my ex-wife: it belongs either to her, or to no one. If the life my ex-wife is living turns out not to belong to my ex-wife then it belongs to no one, in which case my ex-wife is living no one's life. This is a possibility she entertains, credits —without, I may say, the childish sort of dismay this prospect inspires in many people—yet against which she nonetheless rebels. She *acknowledges* the possibility that the life she's living isn't her own life, indeed is no one's life, yet *embraces* the possibility that the life she's living is her own. She chooses to proceed as though she had choice in the matter, chooses to live the life she's living as though it were her own life, hers to choose. Her knitting, then, which others choose to view as a compulsion, I choose to view rather as an expression of the choice she's freely made about herself. Its very extravagance, its oddity —the muffler, according to my kids, that is to *our* kids, is now the size of four school yards, incorporating eighty-eight shades of wool—this knitting's oddity, as I say, seems designed to skew the odds in favour of the life my ex-wife's living being her own life, rather than no one's, an attempt that is by my ex-wife to *weigh in* on the side of idiosyncrasy. My ex-wife seems to me to have chosen for herself a project so outrageous —the knitting of an infinitely large muffler, a muffler without edge or frontier, capable of comforting everyone and everything——as to be inexplicable in any manner other than as an outgrowth, an overflowing of her own life.

This is just me, of course. I may be wrong. And sure, I worry about the kids on their weeks with my ex-wife. Then again, when *don't* I worry about the kids? At least, with her, I know they'll be warm.

Misterioso

You listen to his music, Monk's music, to its broken rhythms, its dislocations, dissonances, its quips and queer silences, its harmonies that pelt down on you like handfuls of thrown pebbles, and you wonder where it all would have gone if he'd never sat down at a piano, Mr. Thelonius Sphere Monk—"Monkey" they called him as a boy—if at six years old he hadn't started picking out tunes on those eighty-eight keys, if there hadn't turned out to be eighty-eight at all but, say, sixty-three, or thirty-seven, or some other such number that meant to him absolutely nothing, if his little fingers hadn't found their way amongst those eighty-eight black and white stepping stones to some hide-out, some cloister, if preachers and faith healers hadn't suffered him to play by their sides, if his little monkey hands had been left idle in his pockets, to fidget with chestnuts and bits of string incapable of releasing any sound. What would have happened to all that weird beauty, you wonder, to those uncanny thoughts, if there'd been no instrument on which to think them, and more, what would have happened to the man destined to choke on those thoughts, to be torn up by them as by a tangle of steel string snarled up in his belly, what would he have muttered to himself as he danced on what street corner bleeding to death inside, and who would have found him in what gutter, body frozen into what mute gesticulation? Was there a moment, you wonder, at which he might have missed his calling, might have turned away from the sound of his own irredeemably unique voice into some terminal silence? Was there such a moment for you? Was there something you might have found, some means, some method for getting all this passionate incoherence *out of you*, some instrument you failed to find or found and failed to recognize? Is it too late?

Smoked Salmon

There are just these fragments of perception, Sara once said to me, *the way they meld and sheer apart.* I'm thinking about this as I lie by the campfire, my head in her lap. This and other things. We're tenting a week at Long Beach as a makeshift honeymoon until we can afford airfare somewhere hotter, and until we're married. Sara's reading to me from a little red book called *The Seven Valleys And The Four Valleys,* a book about the Bahá'í faith, of which neither of us are members, or have any interest in becoming members.

Sara leans forward, gathering firelight for her page. The fine ends of her hair brush my face, each one alone, all together. She has a free hand. I take it, slip one of her fingers into my mouth. I taste smoked salmon. Strange—our salmon wasn't smoked.

I bite down gently.

"Ouch," says Sara.

She's had her hand in amongst the charred wood. And it occurs to me that this is exactly what she meant, this mysterious splicing and fraying of sensations. The salmon, the smoke. Smoked salmon.

"Sara," I say, "Will we always be together?"

"Yes?" she says.

Where did the flavours intermingle? On her finger? In my mouth?

"We could have a dog," I say. "We could call it, Bahá'u'lláh."

Sara giggles. "After passing through the Valley of Knowledge," she reads, "which is the last plane of limitation, the wayfarer cometh to the Valley of Unity and drinketh from the cup of the Absolute, and gazeth on the Manifestations of Oneness. In this station he pierceth the veils of plurality...."

"Pierceth," I murmur. "Pierceth." It's just that I love the sound of it.

Stab

He was born that way, with the knife in his heart, came into this world with the knife sticking into his heart, and sticking also of course *out of* his heart, right out through the wall of his chest: imagine the fun his mom had. Imagine the fun she had getting him out. Not enough to be pushing out a nine-pound-nine-ounce monster of a baby, no, not enough to be extruding this huge *personality*, as she described him right from the start, this enormous *personality*, but to be extruding this enormous personality with a knife sticking out of its heart. Ouch. There was no way to pull it out, they told her, the doctors, no way to pull the knife out of her little boy's heart because to pull it out would amount to stabbing him. To pull it out would destroy him. He hadn't been destroyed when the knife was pushed into him because of course the knife hadn't been pushed into him (though it must, I suppose, at some point have been pushed into his mom). It had been there from the start, that knife, sticking right into him, sticking into his heart. The knife hadn't been stabbed into him, pushed into him, but rather had been pulled into him as he grew. He'd in effect pulled that knife into himself, made it a part of himself as he grew. He'd never been stabbed, yet all his life he'd been walking around with this knife sticking into his heart. To pull the knife out of his heart: this would have amounted to stabbing him. Yet imagine the temptation, for his mom, and later for him, to grab the handle of that knife and pull it out of his heart. What a relief. What a release. This is what his life amounted to, in a sense: one great struggle to resist this temptation, the temptation to take that knife in his own two hands and tug it out of his heart. The temptation to stab himself, free himself once and for all by tugging that knife out of his heart.

A temptation we could hardly expect him to resist forever.

What To Do Next

"But what hurt me most of all," my wife says, "is that even then you didn't cry. Even when you finally realized you were losing me, that I was leaving...." And there it is once more, the throatiness, the choked wet fullness of that reedy voice as it readies for weeping.

I comfort her a while, until she's caught her breath, then I hang up the phone. I go over to the window. Warm air pours in over the sill, heavy with lilac and exhaust. I put my face close to the glass. I look out, but I don't see anything. There's this image forming in my head.

There's a man. A man who's hung on to his wife for years, not through constancy or devotion, as it turns out, but by reducing her to a state of such helplessness and misery that she simply wasn't capable of crawling out the door. A man whose daughter is under the impression she must have been beaten or molested by him, but that it's screwed her up so badly she's blotted it from her mind. A man whose son has a look in his bloodshot eyes each day that says, *jesus god, let me grow up nothing like this man*. A man who considers himself a predator when he desires a woman, a faggot when he misses a friend. A man who's just learned that everything about him, everything he's ever fostered in himself, is exactly what demeans, defiles, destroys the world.

This almost works. My body goes into an impressive seizure of some sort, but it's like a case of the dry heaves: plenty of retching with nothing produced, nothing released. I'm bent over, straining at the air. I'm a mute screaming.

This goes on for a while, then it stops. My eyes have watered with the effort. I blink and look around.

I wonder what to do next.

Session

I believe, and my therapist agrees with me, Dr. Coverdale agrees with me, that there are two therapeutic questions, the question *what's happened to me* and the question *what might I become*, but beyond this point we disagree. While Dr. Coverdale—an able therapist, I believe, her prim, professional manner nicely balanced by her head of mad, red, rasta-like hair—while Dr. Coverdale believes that these questions must be taken in order, that the question *what might I become* must wait upon the answer to the question *what's happened to me*, I personally don't believe this program to be practical. I believe that the question *what's happened to me* is interminable, that it must be circumvented, answered in only the most cursory way and then evaded if the question *what might I become* is ever to be broached. It's my view that many patients, many people, spend their lives, knowingly or unknowingly, grappling with the question *what's happened to me*, never progressing to the question *what might I become*, in fact that almost no one in the history of our civilization has succeeded in posing the question *what might I become*, but that, with the exception of a very few individuals, they've been obsessed with the question *what's happened to me*, ensnared by it, trapped by it, and that Dr. Coverdale is not one of these very few individuals. What's fascinating about our sessions, then, my sessions with Dr. Coverdale—apart, of course, from her hair, her unprecedented hair—is that while she continues to press upon me the question *what's happened to me*, I answer her as though she's gone on to press the question *what might I become*, I address my whole presence to the perfecting of a style which explicitly subverts the question *what's happened to me*, transforming it into the question *what might I become*, and gazing at her hair.

Eddy

At first I'm like, no way.

Eddy, this kid at school with me, in first grade? He's always the one to come up with stuff first. Like back in day care, when we first met? I was missing the nipple like crazy, so he says to me, "Try your thumb. It's almost as good, and it's *yours*, so you can suck it whenever you bloody well please." But I'm all, no way. Then I try it, and as a matter of fact it isn't all that bad. I've been sucking it ever since.

Also, it was Eddy who came up with the idea of refusing to have a dump, back when they were toilet training us, of just holding it in until they asked you for it *nicely*. And it worked. Eddy went five days: he had them grovelling.

Still, this time I'm totally, no *way*.

"I'm telling you, it's your only chance," says Eddy. "I mean, do you *like* it out here? You want back in, don't you? Well, you're going to have to be your *own* daddy this time. Otherwise you're just this big joke, you're just this fluke." Eddy pauses, gives me the look. The I-hope-you're-not-a-*total*-geek look. "You know what to do once he's out of the way, right, once you've got her alone?"

"Oh, yeah, yeah," I say. But as a matter of fact I'm not all that sure.

Hopefully it'll just come to me.

The Kingdom of Heaven 87

Ketchup

The first draft went like this:

Under hypnosis, the patient has recalled a dream in which he visits a "past-life regressionist", who, with the use of hypnosis, purports to lead him into a previous incarnation. In this regressive trance (in the dream, in the trance) he's provided us with the following spoken material:

As you say, Herr Professor Freud, the purpose of the dream is to keep the dreamer asleep. Energies arise and must be discharged lest they arouse us. The dream arouses us in order that we won't be aroused. This is the irony, of course, Herr Professor: I'm trying to awaken myself from a dream whose sole purpose is to keep me asleep. A bad dream, a very bad dream. I cry out, "But Herr Professor, my sister, your wife, what if she hears us?" hoping to awaken myself. But, "Ah, my little Minna, my little vixen," you growl, snuffing out your pipe, unbuttoning your fly. "I'm...I've never," I protest. "You say no," you chuckle, "but I hear only yes, yes, yes...." So this must be what I wanted, what I've always wanted. This must be....

The recollection ends here. In light of the dreamer's propensity for violent sexuality—which of course brought him to us in the first place—the dream may be read straightforwardly enough as wish fulfilment. The scenario allows him to rape, indeed, to rape himself. This interpretation is complicated, however, by the fact that the material was delivered in German—a language of which the patient seems to have no conscious knowledge—and that it draws on sophisticated psychoanalytic concepts (not to mention historical speculation, as regards Freud's alleged incestuous relationship with Minna Bernays, his wife's sister) of which the patient (an unemployed construction worker) cannot be shown to have any understanding.

Which is odd, since I'd only intended to write out a shopping list. So the second draft goes like this:

carrots
light bulbs (60w)
ketchup

Violence

I'm jotting you this note, Dr. Pound, Irwin—may I call you Irwin? —I'm jotting you this note to signify that I'm *opting out* of a visit to your office, a visit which you've urged Isabelle to insist upon so urgently. You wish to see us together: it's the logical next step in her therapy. You wish *her* therapy to become *our* therapy. I understand. Nonetheless, here I am opting out, even as I support Isabelle in opting in, indeed, even as I continue to foot the bill.

No explanation is required of me, of course, but I'm inclined to offer one anyway. Perhaps it'll amuse you, even enlighten you —concerning my hang-ups, my *issues,* if nothing else. The most ready interpretation of my behaviour, certainly, is that I'm a coward, that I haven't the fortitude to risk the radical intimacy of the therapeutic process. I acknowledge this interpretation. I grant it to you. With your indulgence, let me now serve up another, which has the virtue at least that it's a little longer, a little more complex, that it makes my refusal look a little more *interesting*.

What else is there for us to do, after all, Dr. Irwin, but interpret, but offer interpretation? This is our *business,* isn't it, the human business? Certainly it's *your* business. Your specialty is violence, I understand: what's violence but the imposition of an interpretation on somebody else (as I'm imposing this one on you, for instance)? Isn't this also the nature of therapy? I've seen Isabelle through a dozen therapies, so far, each a new reading of the labyrinth, the baffling imbroglio of her *self,* so-called, each masquerading as a reflection of the true nature of that self. Each in truth only one more interpretation. Not false, not final. One of many. The goal of each of her therapists has been to convince her of one caricature of herself, to press it upon her, through whatever means—manual or mental, on the couch or on the table —have proven most effective.

If you've bought all this so far—as I don't for a moment imagine you have—you'll have reached the conclusion that *therapy is violence.* Kindly offered, in most cases, a violence intended to eradicate the imprint of some former violence, some former version of the self inflicted by more savage means. But violence nonetheless. Don't get me wrong, I'm under no illusion that such violence can be avoided. In refusing your treatment I'm only exercising my right to *choose the violence* inflicted upon me, indeed, to choose to be the *source* of that violence. This is a dicey project. I'm perplexed by it, easily thrown off. It's a delicate

The Kingdom of Heaven 89

violence I'm working upon myself, Dr. Irwin, and I'm frankly terrified that your very expertise, your practised torturer's technique....

So we're back again to my fear, my cowardliness. Which is, I suspect, right where you want us to be. Fortunately for you I'm frightened also of the violence that's already been done to Isabelle, of the cruel version of herself abiding in her flesh. And I miss her in bed. So I give my blessing (or would, if I were ever asked for it) to the exercise of your powers upon her.

Please find enclosed, then, a cheque for this week's session, and for next.

Yours sincerely,

Look At Me

I went to the doctor and I went, *"Look at me."*
"Very slight balding," he said. "Not abnormal."
And I went, *"But I'm a woman!"*
"Nothing to worry about," he said.

So he did ultraviolet radiation on me, and vitamins, and thyroid hormones, and steroids. And none of it worked, of course, and I felt so incredibly stupid by this time and I finally had to tell him, *"It's me. I'm pulling it out. Me!"*

He looked at me, and he sort of blinked. "Oh," he said. "You should have told me."

"Of course I should have told you!" I said. *"That's what I mean!"*

And he blinked again, and got out a piece of paper and wrote something on it and handed me the piece of paper. "I want you to speak to this person. She's a doctor too, okay?"

And I went, *"Okay!"*

And I did, I spoke to her many times, the doctor, and since then things have changed. For a while I pulled out even more hair than ever. I pulled it out one strand at a time, I pulled it out in big hanks, twirled it around my fingers until it was well twisted and tangled and yanked it out with a pop. I started going bald in patches. People thought I had cancer. They gave me these pitying looks. I liked it for a while, then I didn't like it. I bought a wig, but it was very red, redder than I imagined when I bought it, and I refused to wear it. Bill said anything was better than having to see my scalp. Mother offered to buy me another one, she pleaded with me, but I went, *"I thought you were supposed to love me for what I am,"* and I hung up.

Then I started pulling out Bill's hair. I don't know what gave me the idea. It was a stroke of genius, I guess, I have one every once in a while. I'm lying there beside him in bed one night, just listening to him snore, as usual, and there's all this beautiful hair on the pillow glistening in the moonlight. I reach out and take a strand. I tug. Bill snorts, squirms a bit, then goes right on sleeping. So I pull out another. And so on.

Bill doesn't wake up while I'm doing this, exactly, but he dreams. He tells me about his dreams in the morning, sometimes, about having big needles pushed into his brain to steal his thoughts (Bill has many thoughts, so he says, and he likes to keep them), or being staked out on an ant-hill by Iroquois and having honey smeared on his head, ants gouging into his scalp with their little pincer-mouths. And I feel badly about this, and I feel even worse when I see him peering into the mirror in his pyjamas, poor Bill, wondering what's happened to all his gorgeous golden locks (which are going a little grey, to tell the truth, what's left of them).

On the other hand, I'm starting to sleep much better myself, these nights, deep dreamless sleeps. If one of us has to go bald, better off him than me, I figure. Besides, I can't help feeling good when I see Bill seeing me again, when I notice him noticing the way my thick dark curls are coming back in, almost as though he wants to touch them.

Cut Off

I'm not saying I'll never cut it off, Son, after all who knows what the future holds, what deed or for that matter thought of yours might cause me to cut it off, might force me to cut it off. My dad never cut mine off, clearly, but that's not to say there weren't close calls, that I didn't give him cause. That's not to say I didn't ask for it. What I'm saying is that I know what you're going through, Son. I know what it is to live with that terror, the terror of having it cut off. I think by now you know, though, that there's something worse, something even more terrifying than having it cut off. Something that's in fact already happened to you. You put up with the terror of what might happen, in fact you embrace that terror, insist on that terror, rather than face your grief, which is nothing after all but the terror of what's already happened to you. You live in terror of having it cut off since that's preferable to the alternative, which is to live in grief. You'd rather live in terror of what might happen than live in terror of what's happened. What is it? What's happened? I think you've noticed, Son. I never had mine cut off, clearly, I'm sure that's perfectly clear to you—here, look!—but as for your mother.... I'm pretty sure you've noticed. There's nothing there to cut off —it's been cut off. Your mother's had it cut off, Son. What, precisely, did she have cut off? What was there that isn't there now? You, Son. She had *you* cut off. You were cut off, you're *cut off*. This is what you grieve, Son, or rather this is what you *would* grieve if you weren't so busy being terrified. This is why you keep yourself so busy being terrified of what might happen, so you won't have time to be terrified of what's happened: that you've been cut off, that *you're what's been cut off*. I know you've noticed, Son....

You haven't? Oh. Well then, never mind.

April

I was chaise lounging it out on my back deck, soaking up some of that musty early spring light. I'd taken off my t-shirt: a cool breeze ruffled the hair on my chest, goose-pimpling my sun-warmed skin. Daffs were thrusting up out of the damp dirt in pots all around me. The whole world had gone faintly and serenely phallic. For the first time in months—since Jerry's winter solstice party, as a matter of fact—I felt good.

My book was a hardback, a big thick beauty. I'd had it on reserve at the library for ages. Its appearance that day was just one more blessing—one more signal from the cosmos, Jerry would say. *Mystery and Cruelty*, the book was called, a new collection of essays by Robert Licht, the American cultural critic. It's an examination of the kinds of barbarity that can attend upon an infatuation with uncertainty, with the unknown. It's about the heartlessness of the seeker.

I was lying on my back, the book soaring wingspread at arm's length above me. I turned a page: a slip of paper darted out and dead-leafed it down onto my chest. I lowered the book, left it straddling my belly. I picked up the paper. It was a reserve slip. *James Tietzen. Card #9423. Phone #656-2121.* Last person to turn these pages.

I closed my eyes. What kind of a man would he be, this James Teitzen? A man, first of all—since he could handle Licht—cerebral enough to have experienced the intoxication, the seductive vertigo of rigorous irony. A man obsessed with an intellectual quest, yet appalled by the cost of his own single-mindedness. A man who understood the chimeric nature of truth, the density of suffering. He'd also—it was spring, recall, and I'd just been alone through a long winter, under yellow, crystalline snow which had failed to keep me warm—be young, and healthy, and looking for a man like me.

All this—insanely, miraculously—turns out to be the case. I called James that day, and related the things I've related here. This is key to the whole experience as far as I can discern, this faithful rendering of my particular state at that particular moment. James responded as though he received such calls every day, or rather, as though he'd never received one, and had always wondered why.

Jerry would say—has said—I told you so. *You get what you need*, he says. I don't believe that. I believe something, but that isn't it.

A Little Paradox

You read in Mumon's *Mumonkan*, his *Gateless Gate*, a paperback copy on loan to you from the new woman in your life, Margaret—Meg, she's got you calling her—who's into the eastern stuff that's always mystified you so much (you're really just ploughing through this to please her):

As for those who try to understand through other people's words, they are striking at the moon with a stick; scratching a shoe, whereas it's the foot that itches.

And all of a sudden, you *get it*.

Revision

In his memoirs, as I recalled, Elias Canetti had confessed to his despair at the destruction, the conflagration with which his novel, *Auto Da Fé*, (at the time entitled, in manuscript form, *Kant Catches Fire*) had come to an end. This was the book in which all books were incinerated, a literary catastrophe to which Canetti himself, of course, was party, and for which he bore enormous guilt. A bizarre, brutal piece of writing, the novel conjured a constellation of crippled and benighted characters, all of whom failed unfailingly to comprehend one another and the nature of their own delusions. The comedy came to an end only when its main character, Kant (later Kien, which is to say, *kindling*), a brilliant, brittle, monumentally repressed sinologist, set himself and his massive library alight, sacrificing knowledge upon the altar of ignorance and cruelty. When he'd done with it (at about the time of the emergence of the little mustachioed Aryan monster, some years before the latest great conflagration in Europe), Canetti—the grand inquisitor, as it were—reported feeling just awful.

Then why? Why had he gone through with it? Other endings, after all, had offered themselves up, many of them holding out the promise, to Canetti, of a Volume Two, even Three. Yet he opted for apocalypse. Under some sort of compulsion, some irresistible madness, he set a match to his own highly combustible world.

I was just then poised to begin ending my own first and (who knew?) possibly last novel—had not Canetti himself called it quits after one? —and was feeling oppressed by the responsibility of playing lone deity to my little universe. My problem was much like the one that had confronted Canetti's great friend, Robert Musil, in concluding (as he never did) his magnum opus: do they or don't they? The long lost sister and brother who find in one another their "own self love", long lost aspects of themselves which might at last be embraced: do they make love, or don't they? In my case the pair were half-brother and half-sister, offering one another, it struck me, the perfect, most perfectly erotic combination of familiarity and strangeness, difference and identity. The question *do they or don't they* had already in this instance been answered: my half-siblings had bedded down halfway through the manuscript. Now, in the closing chapters, they'd discovered themselves pregnant. The question before me, as creator and judge, was the following: was the child *okay*, or was it *not okay*? The offspring of this half-incestuous love: beautiful babe, or monster? Yet already I knew—already a monster had been conceived in me, was drawing dark life from the swollen placenta in my skull. Not for me, I considered, even to wonder why. Only for me to muster the courage to induce the labour of the birth.

I was at my desk, as a matter of fact, deep-breathing and sharpening pencils, at the moment I got the call from Mel, Maggie's husband, my sister's husband. (It was Maggie, incidentally, who'd turned me on to Canetti in the first place, who turned me on to Musil.) I'd been expecting the call—the baby was well past due.

"I'm at the hospital," said Mel. "We wanted you to know right away."

"Wait a sec," I said. "Just hang on a sec." I had to slow him down. They frightened me, these words coming at me out of nowhere, already as they emerged so far beyond revision.

Weather

The trouble of course is that now that I can say cancer, or *cumulus*, say, now that I can say cumulus I haven't any idea what it is *not* to know how to say cumulus, if you see what I mean. I no longer know what it is not to know under what sort of conditions, under what sort of sky to say cumulus. What sort of sky was it before, this sky under which I now say *cumulus*? What was a cumulus cloud to me before it was a *cumulus cloud*? is what I'm wondering, but wondering this I'm already wondering about a *cumulus cloud*, if you see what I mean. It's too late. It's not possible any longer, it'll never again be possible for me to wonder about a cumulus cloud that isn't already a *cumulus cloud*. The question, "What was a cumulus cloud before it was a *cumulus cloud*?" has no meaning for me except as a gesture of nostalgia, a pointing back towards a past perfectly *socked in*, if you see what I mean. By the time I've thought of a cumulus cloud, by the time a cumulus cloud has come scudding into my mind it's already a *cumulus cloud* that's come scudding, just as it might have been a *cirrus cloud*, or for that matter a *cirrocumulus undulatus cloud* that came scudding. What was it to me before it was a *cirrocumulus undulatus cloud*? I wonder. Of what did it consist, for me, before it consisted of ice crystals condensing, falling, teased by ten-mile high winds into great rippling filaments, strands, streamers? Of what did it remind me before it reminded me of waves of sand in the shallows of a beach? What did I see in it before I saw an instability, a shuddering in the air? What did it mean to me before it meant a change in the weather? What was I asking before I was asking these questions?

Stranger

It's like the night she first tried getting pregnant, I suspect, tried letting him in, my dad, her late husband—not late at all, at the time, but on the whole early, much too early—tried taking him right into her womb. After all the latex and rubber, the condoms and calendars, after the *coitus* that was so often *interruptus*, how strange it must have been to lie down with him quite naked, curl up in his arms unhurried, unarmed. A new woman in the grasp of a new man. A treachery, a tryst —sweet transgression. And how strange, after all the prayed-for periods, the promises never to take even the slightest risk again, to be pleading to be *late*, this time, pleading for her blood to be dammed up within her, to form a pool, a hot pond in which some new creature might invent itself.... Strange. Inviting life in, all at once, after so many moons spent shutting it out. Not her life, not his. Life anonymous, unrefined. Faceless—who could yet have imagined anything like me, anything as weirdly *featured*, as *particular* as me? Begging for invasion, is what she was doing, begging to be haunted, possessed. Begging, after two decades' endeavouring to sculpt herself into a thing indivisible, to be cracked in two. Shattered.

Or like that first night in the hospital, two years ago now, the night we told her to *wet the bed*, essentially, empty herself into the little metal pan. Scolded her, as a matter of fact, for holding it in, just as she must have been scolded as a little girl for *failing* to hold it in —just as I scold my little girl, now, for failing to hold it in. What a shock for her, for my mother, to discover just how well the lesson had been learned, how her whole body, her whole being clutched at itself, refused to let go. *Relax*, we told her. *Release*. As easy, after six decades of decency, to curse all at once out loud, howl in desire or despair, bare her body to the stares of strangers.

Yes, a little like that, it must be, dying, learning to die. *Life is everlasting, and I am not*. Like taking a breath under water, talking with her mouth full. Like leaping without first looking, opening the door, home all alone, to someone she knows she's never seen before.

"Hello?" she moans, eyes straining into that darkness.

"I'm here, I'm here," I murmur. But I'm interrupting

Second Person

"You, you, you, you, you," you used to whisper, moan. The ultimate pillow talk, consoling me as I sank into my body, sank my body into yours, disappeared. Reassuring me that it was *me*, that I could do you like no one. That the ecstatic body was not the moribund body. Our first night, in your father's old room at your mother's place—the forget-me-nots, the must—and every other night since. Wet words in my ear: a prayer offered up to the dying. Very sweet.

But of course now you've gone and done it with him, him, him, him. The same thing, the only thing. And whispered the same sweet nothing, the same loving lie. Second person pronoun: the last word you hear as you vanish.

The Scientific Method

The object of our experiment was in effect to establish whether or not "Mikey" (#1107) could be made mortal—could be induced to believe, that is, that he was an object, that he was destined to die, that he'd *lose himself* in the final event, just as he'd lost his dear mate "Margitt" (#1113)—and if so to observe his behaviour under the influence of this delusion. To this end we set about prying Mikey free of himself, employing his rudimentary chimp-tongue to talk him up into his head and then *out into the world*, out into his now-empty cage. From this vantage, we knew, he'd before long glance back and glimpse himself, recognize himself as *other*. In time he'd begin to ponder—albeit in his limited, simian way—the possibility that he might one day be robbed of himself just as he'd been robbed of others. As he'd been robbed, for instance, of his dear mate Margitt. Only others die, of course—we took this as axiomatic. (In the event of Mikey's decease, after all, Mikey can hardly be said to have lost Mikey, suffered the loss of Mikey. Only the rest of us can be said to have suffered this loss.) The question we posed ourselves, then, was strictly whether or not Mikey could be made to suffer from the *fear* of losing Mikey. Again, only others die: making Mikey mortal was therefore a matter of making him *other*, removing him from himself, luring him out of himself into his now-empty cage. It was a matter of turning him into an object with respect to himself, disrupting his pure subjectivity—his immortality.

This was the object of the second stage of our experiment. We'd demonstrated already that Mikey was capable of *sadness*—a significant experimental result, incidentally, which more than justified, so far as we were concerned, the sacrifice of his dear mate Margitt. It remained only to demonstrate that he was capable of *sickness*, in the sense of neurosis—capable, that is, of mortality. That we failed in this attempt, that Mikey died as he'd lived—immortal—is a serious but not fatal setback for our project. More funding will come through in the end, no doubt; another suitable subject will be secured. In the meantime our corresponding work with children continues. Indeed, a report has just recently come in concerning a child of merely four years old, believed already to be on the verge of mortality.

So far as we're concerned, then, there's no cause for panic.

Block

My point of view in this piece, the piece I've begun but not yet finished, the piece I'm *unable* to finish, as you're so fond of putting it, is that I'm not actually unable but *unwilling* to finish it. That's the whole *point* of the piece, for goodness' sake. The point of the piece is that despite my own efforts to wrap it up, this piece, I'll never actually allow myself to wrap it up, I'll be forever thwarting myself in these efforts. Surely you've understood this. From the start my contention has been that I as creator, as a creature struggling to create, *block myself*, that we all block ourselves, create insurmountable barriers to the completion of any piece in order to be spared completing it, in order to be spared completing *ourselves*—in order to be spared dying. To finish is to die. This is my point of departure, as you've known from the start. I argue from Kant, or at least I *will* argue from Kant when I get to that part of the piece, or at least I'll argue from Fichte who argues from Kant —pile them up, you've taught me, one mind on top of another—who argues that it's imperative that we perfect ourselves, that this process of perfecting ourselves takes forever, and therefore that we're immortal. If it *didn't* take forever, this process of perfecting ourselves, we *wouldn't* be immortal. Get it? "Because my work must be accomplished," argues Fichte, "because I have to fulfil my vocation, there is no limit to my life. I am eternal." Fichte *wouldn't* be eternal, in other words, if Fichte's work *were* to be accomplished. The accomplishment of Fichte's work, the end of Fichte's work would be the *end of Fichte*. The goal of the work therefore, of any work which is a movement towards completion, towards totality, is an endless postponement of completion, an endless putting off of totality. This is my perspective in the piece, as you know quite well, the piece you're suddenly so keen on me completing. Surely you can see that to complete such a piece, to complete a piece the point of which is that completion means death, would be insane, completely insane. To force me to complete such a piece would be tantamount to murder. To *cut off funding* for such a piece would be to kill its author, as the piece itself makes clear, or at least is in the process of making clear. Nothing's quite clear as yet, I confess, nor can it ever be quite clear. Nothing's complete, nothing....

The Kingdom of Heaven 102

A Third Thing

What I want to think is something else, something other than what I'm thinking. What I want to think is in all cases something else. Just now, for instance, I'm thinking how hard it is to be alone and thinking, and this isn't what I want to be thinking, this is precisely what I don't want to be thinking. Whenever I'm alone I'm thinking how hard it is to be alone and thinking, which isn't what I want to be thinking, yet the only way to think otherwise is to force myself to think how much worse, how infinitely much worse it would be if I were with someone else, and vice versa, if you see what I mean. But I don't want to think either of these things, either that I'm alone and don't want to be alone, or that I'm alone and thankful I'm alone, I want to think a third thing, which is unthinkable. This third thing is unthinkable precisely because to think it would be to concentrate, and this is precisely what I can't do, for the reason that I'm alive, and that to be alive is precisely to be unable to concentrate. This is what it means to be alive, to be unable to concentrate. This is what I've always thought of as "the tragedy of life", when I've been able to think of it at all, the tragedy or the comedy, or some other thing, some third thing, of which I'm unable to think, for the reason that I'm alive, alive or dead, or some third thing.

Crush

Don't marry up in the world, Mom used to say, but don't marry down either. Come as near to marrying yourself as possible without getting incestuous. She'd had a close call herself: Dad was a second cousin once removed. He was a wife-beating, daughter-fondling monster, but he was her kind of people: well-to-do, upstanding, godfearing. I knew she wasn't going to be wild about Francis. The only question was whether he was he too high up her Chain of Being or too low down, whether he tended more to the archangel or the beast. On the one hand his folks were stinking rich, on the other they were church-mad to the point of vulgarity. A little piety goes a long way, Mom used to say.

Anyhow, by the time our gang hit puberty, back there in Assisi, it was clear that Francis was equal to none of us. He dressed so strangely, and he spoke in such strange tongues. The other girls thought he was kooky—I thought he was the sweetest thing on God's earth. When his hands and feet bled I'd hold them to my breasts (the little buds I had at the time) wishing there were actual wounds so I could bind them up. When he preached to the animals I concentrated till I thought my head would split, hoping to be swept up in the great divine unity of his love. What a boy! Once I found him naked in a clearing at night, stroking himself, moaning at the sky. Another time I found him balling his eyes out over a trampled snail. These weren't the kind of things I could talk over with Mom.

What I'd like to know is, why couldn't I have fallen for a nice normal boy, like Nathan, for instance? I'm positive he liked me. He was much better looking than Francis, and he was captain of all sorts of teams. Thomas was soft on me too—Madeleine saw him staring all through communion. But no, I had to get a crush on the school holy fanatic and spend the rest of my days following him around in a cowl. Now I have only my poverty left to me, my poverty and my great, ludicrous love. If I'd just listened to Mom. Then again, I guess you never do. If I've followed anyone in the family it's got to be Gran. She married a crazy too—he'd have been a saint by now, I bet, if Gran hadn't gotten with child. I should be so lucky. But of course, none of this is in our hands. None of it. Do you want to know something funny? I love Francis, Francis loves God and now God, I find out, loves me. There's just no end to it anywhere.

Speed Of Light

Flipping through her notebook, on the look-out for clues: *Uncertainty isn't simply a quirk of the human condition, but an intrinsic feature of this universe. The act of observation is a part of the world, and alters the world irrevocably....* The grand, mystic tone: hers, or his? Good physics, or just a part of the seduction? *Under the pull of its own gravity, the universe curls inwards, forming a finite, unbounded sphere in four dimensions....* Gibberish. Abstruse nothings murmured into her ear across a crowded classroom. "Ms. Pebbles, if I might just throw you over the couch after class...."

It was time for her to get out in the world again, I knew that. Children would have kept her busy, perhaps even content, but there were no children, were to be none, and that was that. So, no choice but to broaden herself. *Humanity is stranded roughly half way in between micro and macro, quark and red giant. On this middle ground we're at home. Our old ideas are impregnable until they run into the very large, the very small, the very fast, the very dense....*

What's most fascinating about our old ideas, according to June's notes, is that they're almost right, or rather, that they're completely wrong, yet they furnish us with convincing answers. We're granted the limiting case. We can stay home if we want to. *"Now" is a local phenomenon. Time isn't absolute, nor is motion, nor stillness....* There are clues, subtle mockings of our ignorance, but we're free to ignore them. There must have been clues. Something about the way she sighed when I entered her, or didn't sigh. Some aberration in the light of her eyes. It would have been a slight thing. She was not fooling around, after all, with nearly every man on the face of the earth. In fact there was only one man with whom she was not not fooling around. She was virtually faithful, yet she was completely unfaithful. How could this be? *The decline of the old paradigm began with the recognition of certain slight, almost unnoticeable inconsistencies in the behaviour of light....*

In almost every case we don't die, yet the fact that we die once renders us wholly mortal. Only exception is truth, only anomaly. Truth is the lone thread which, tugged just so, causes the little world to unravel, leaving us alone in the big one. The big world is cold, but infinitely beautiful. June lies in the next room, staring at the ceiling. Light moves towards us from some distant star, curves towards us through space at one hundred and eighty-six thousand miles per second.

Soon it will be here.

Yors

The way it usually works is that one of us, Jimmy or Bong or I, brings in an idea, you know, a theme, a chorus, a chord progression, whatever, and then the three of us, like, jam on it. You know? We just let things happen. We're sort of, whatever happens, happens, you know? Like with "Yors", on the *Ekstasis* cd. "Yors" was the tune that put us over the top. Half a million copies. So what happened was that Bong had been having trouble with his old lady, you know how it is, and he was, like, totally bummed, and he's suddenly all, I want to *belong* to her, I hope he's not going to freak when he hears this, no, he's cool, he's cool. I mean, if you can't share this stuff then what's the point, right? So anyway, it comes to him that this whole thing of wanting to be hers is really about *not* wanting to be *his*, if you see what I mean, about wanting to be rid of himself, to be disburdened of himself, to repudiate his own *radical finiteness*, I think he put it, to become nothing, to die in a way, to die the death, the death-in-life, so that he could receive himself back from her as renewed being, over and over again, at every instant to give himself up and receive himself. That's *ekstasis*, you see, a standing outside oneself. It was a whole dread thing, dread of being a self, dread of failing to be a self, you know. I don't know. Anyway, it sounded like an E minor kind of a thing to me, so I just started laying down some bass and Bong picked it up. The whole rhythmic business, ba-bum, ba-bum-ba, was his idea. Then Jimmy came in, like, scatting at first, you know, getting the feel of it, and then the lyrics just happened. They just happened. The whole "swallow me, swallow me" thing—well, what I'm saying is that you have to take it in context. Anyway, Bong's back with his old lady now, so that's, you know, a really hopeful thing. That's part of it too, I mean, everything's part of it....

Does that answer your question?

Mine

Strange, now, to conceive of it as my own, as a singular condition, when I'd always thought it to be universal. Has this made it any easier to bear, or harder still? An unanswerable question. Rather, a question that can only be answered endlessly, an answering that can't cease once it's begun.

But it didn't. It didn't begin. Or it began with memory, this condition. It's always been there, so present as to be barely detectable. A natural assumption, then, that it was natural, that everybody started with it, that it started with everybody. That it was common to us all. And to learn, now, by accident as it were, through a casual comment, a time-of-the-day sort of comment, that at least one other person has never felt it, that several others, most others, perhaps all others are only puzzled, uncomprehending, that this feeling——which I must acknowledge now as a pain—occurs in me and me alone. A pain, yes, a throbbing—almost, when I come to think of it, an agony. Nonfatal. Incurable. A grief which I'd taken for *being*, but which I discover now to be only *being myself*. Weirdly, irredeemably mine.

And this is what I offer you.

Leaving

I've left a time or two myself, abandoned big relationships, parents, friends, lovers, wife, but none of my departures holds a candle to hers, to Lynn's. This has got to be the definitive disappearance. Here's the message she left behind, on the fridge beneath the panda-bear magnet:

I haven't left you for another man. I haven't left you for a woman. You'll hear rumours—I've heard one already, from Barb, a beauty. They'll be lies. No one could replace you, Benny, so I've left you for no one. Get it? There's only one thing I've ever missed with you, and that's missing. I'm leaving you to hollow myself out, to get on with the life of an angel, the life of lack. I'll learn to be silent, to live with an open, empty mouth. To be full of hunger....

Give Maynard some extra cuddles, okay? He'll be bereft. I'll send along Puppy Chow payments every month. I've just taken him for his walk, the big circuit around W. Park....

There's so much to start missing....

Love Forever,
Lynn

This, surely, is leaving in its purest form. This is life transformed into art: the thing conjured precisely so it can be snatched away. The object employed to trap the awareness so that emptiness will linger there like an after-image, in the fragile shape of the departed. So that we can apprehend *what-was-the-beloved*. And trace this longing back to its source, to the corresponding lack that's the heart of us.

Maynard knows. He trots around the apartment, nosing at the spaces left behind by her belongings. Whining at the scent of her in the abandoned air.

The Art of the Fugue

It's always the same. He takes his seat at the piano gingerly, solemnly, like a man kneeling down to pray. The room is stark, sun-streaked—he's alone there with his devotion. Devotion to nothing, or at least to nothing he can name. Devotion to devotion. It's not necessary for him to know the object of this devotion, even if the object of this devotion is nothing, only to know that without this devotion he himself is nothing.

It's always the same. Fingertips to the keys of the piano he begins to *play*, move his fingertips over the keys of the piano, the black and white keys, in the pattern of his devotion, the pattern which is precisely his devotion. It's no longer necessary for him to press down the keys, hasn't been necessary for many years—the music is implied by the motion of his fingertips. Besides, this silent praising allows him to listen in on the life next door, the shrieking of the children, the chiding of the adults, the yapping of the dog, all of which serves to *put off* his ecstasy, to *delay* that motion by which his whole being merges with the motion of his fingertips, by which he himself becomes identical with the act of his devotion. This in turn delays the moment at which his vision will begin to blur, then to vibrate, to shatter into jagged shards of brilliant colour, the moment at which agony will take root behind his eyes.

It's always the same. The aura forming at the periphery of his vision, gradually obscuring the world, bringing with it the spark of discomfort that will flare, soon enough, into flame, a cold crackling fire of pain. It will leave him, during the next twelve hours or so, draped over the couch across the room from his piano, cold cloth over his face turning tepid, which he'll cool each time he staggers into the bathroom to vomit. By the following day the pain will have given way to exhaustion, and to a boundless melancholy. He'll feel, in the depths of this melancholy, that this melancholy is a sin, or rather that his love of this melancholy is a sin, his giving in to the seduction of this melancholy, its languid allure, its ability to set him apart, above, beyond. And this irony too will give him pleasure, the irony that this devotion to creation sets him apart from creation, that his engagement in the act of devotion alienates him absolutely, elevating him with bliss and pain, and he'll feel that this pleasure too is sin, and that the only remedy, the only conceivable salvation is in the act of self-negation, the act of devotion, and he'll long for the moment he's strong enough once again to cross the room and take his seat at the piano.

Codeine

    This pill, this little pill I've just popped is a lie. This is the truth. Truth isn't a headache, precisely, but something born out of a labouring head, an aching head. What's born out of this aching head is truth, one of two truths: that I have a head (Frederic Nietzsche), that I haven't a head (Simone Weil). Two sufferers, two truths. Two headaches, two heads: a head which is everything (Nietzsche), a head which is nothing (Weil). A head which is nothing but the constant overcoming, the constant consuming of head (Nietzsche), a head which is nothing but the constant undermining, the constant eradication of head (Weil). A headache inflating a head (Nietzsche), a headache annihilating a head (Weil). A head replacing God (Nietzsche), a head getting out of the way of God (Weil). A plenum (Nietzsche), a vacuum (Weil). A capitation (Nietzsche), a decapitation (Weil). A heading (Nietzsche), a beheading (Weil). Madness (Nietzsche), death (Weil).... *For chrissake, when will it kick in? It's like I'm being torn in two. It's like I'm being torn in two.*

Powaqa

You get the idea for your new body from a library book your wife's left lying around (can she possibly read all this stuff?) about the Hopi Indians. It's there beside the bed: it'll take your mind off things. You're too weak to lift it, so you prop it on your belly, grasping its outspread wings in hands cold and bony as talons.

You flip to a section headed "The Sorcery Of The Eye", find yourself reading about a kind of witch, or *powaqa*, known as a *two-hearts* (your previous body you got from the X-rays your doctor showed you, five months back; the body before that from a Charles Atlas ad on the back of a Spiderman comic, fifty some-odd years ago). A *two-hearts*, you read, is just that, a person with two hearts, more specifically a human heart and an animal heart. A *two-hearts* can shift forms, human to animal, animal to human, by leaping through a certain ceremonial hoop. On this you'll improvise. The real challenge will be to cultivate that other heart, to conjure a second pulse, an animal pulse in this all-too-human body.

You close your eyes—you can barely keep them open these days. You envision it at about the level of your umbilicus, this second heart. A smaller heart, but pounding slowly and steadily. Pounding at the pace of your wingbeats, blood rushing through its valves at the speed of the sky rushing through your feathers. You wheel, circle; you're all attention. Your head swivels, aiming an eye at the earth below. You're on the look-out for the body, the fallen body, on the look-out for yourself. The moment the human heart falters and stops, this will be the moment to spring through the hoop, to shift into that other body, the vulture body, to fall on yourself, rend, consume yourself, and rise....

When your wife gets back from the drugstore she'll find what she's been preparing herself to find for all these months. She'll find a tatter or two of clothing, a faint trace of blood, perhaps a feather. She'll find nothing.

Part

It's not exactly true that he dies of the truth, the character I'm playing, that he dies of discovering the truth and of telling the truth, the way he's been hoping, but that he dies of discovering that the truth has been discovered, that the truth has been told. He dies of discovering that the world as he knows it, the world he's been inhabiting, is inhabited already by the truth. This discovery kills him. He's been hoping, in fact he's been counting on the fact—without being quite aware of it, which is the challenge of the part—that the world as it exists couldn't possibly exist alongside the truth, couldn't survive the truth. He's been counting on the fact that this world will be obliterated, razed by the truth, and that a new world will be raised up out of these ruins. In time, however, he reads the writing on the wall. He glances up, and without meaning to, reads the writing on the wall. This is when he discovers the truth. The truth is that the truth has been discovered. This discovery obliterates him. He's sitting on the toilet towards the end of the final act, that is to say *I'm* sitting on the toilet towards the end of the final act, pants down around my ankles, grunting and groaning in the effort to void my bowels—one way to get a mention in the press—when I glance up and read the writing on the wall. "To love truth means to endure the void," it says—I read it out loud, as though I'm reciting some bit of potty humour—"and as a result, to accept death. Truth is on the side of death. S.W." As I say, it's not this truth that kills him, or rather this part of the truth, this final part of the truth, but the discovery that this truth already exists, that the world he lives in has already withstood the truth, will continue to withstand the truth, as he himself must now withstand the truth. This truth he can't withstand. The truth he can withstand, but not the truth about the truth, which is that the world can withstand it, indeed that *he* can withstand it. There's no way for him to withstand this truth.

This is the way I play the part, anyway, the only way I can stand it.

Pulp Fiction

We pick up her story (writes the narrator) in the so-called middle ages. She's part of the fibrous wall of a cell deep in the heartwood of a massive hemlock in a stand of North American rainforest, one molecule amongst many. A cellulose molecule, to be precise—and why not?—a great chain of glucosides, nine hundred and ninety-nine of them, each an hexagonal structure, six carbon atoms, ten hydrogen atoms, five oxygen atoms. Nine hundred and ninety-nine snakes, each dutifully swallowing its own tail....

For quite a few hundred years, nothing happens. Nothing worthy at least of a narrator's attention. Our molecule experiences life only vicariously, by way of the whisper of sap through the surrounding cells (she herself being purely structural), a muffled murmur which brings to her images of a great, succulent brightness far above, a rich wet darkness below. Otherwise her peace is undisturbed, but for the distant percussion, now and then, of a woodpecker at work under the tree's distant bark, faint hint at mortality.

But when death comes it's massive, mechanical. A roaring, a grinding, and then an eery sort of acidic invasion. She's stunned by the violence of all this, but even more stunned to discover that she's survived it, that this isn't to be death after all, but transformation. She bobs in her vat of pulp, dazed, twisted, indubitably herself. What next?

Bleached, wrung out, pancaked, she comes off the roll virginally white, to be chopped, scored with lines, and bound into a notebook. This notebook falls into the hands of a would-be author, a middle-aged high-school biology teacher with pretensions to creativity. Bill, is his name. He hasn't actually created anything just yet, our Bill, but is busy compiling an encyclopedia of quotations on the topic of creativity. On our little complex carbohydrate's page he scribbles the following:

"Art has two constant, unending concerns: it always meditates on death and thus always creates life." Boris Pasternak, as cited in N. O. Brown's Love's Body, *as cited in L. Wofley's "Repression's Rainbow", collected in R. Pearce's* Critical Essays On Thomas Pynchon, *given to me by my darling Pat on my fiftieth birthday (so much past, so soon!)....*

So many pages, she reflects, so many books, so many of my fibrous brethren bound and chained so that these fools....

She's a poky thinker, so she gets no further with this thought before she's *recycled* (the encyclopedist having peremptorily given up the ghost, or at least given up his project), returned to the vat to be repulped. For her next incarnation (a step up the Karmic ladder as far as she's concerned) she finds herself part of a postage stamp, at the tip of a stag's antler on a stamp on a postcard bearing a photographic image of a rainforest, light-mottled, streamered with moss, on the flip-side of which is neatly printed:

Dear Angie,
Wish you were here—wish I were too, but the fact is that I picked this up in the heart of the heart of the city....
I do too love you too.
William

Next (back down the ladder) she's buried in a sheet of newsprint, bearing details of the trial of a man accused of multiple murder, and more, of using his victims' skin—as was the fashion at one time in Germany, it seems—to fashion lamp shades, which as we all know ought rather to be fashioned out of *paper*.... Then (upwards) she's part of a party hat, purple, briefly crowning the head of a giggling nonagenarian on his birthday (lawn bowling, out for pizza...).

These are the past lives she remembers: no way to know, now, what incarnations have been lost, slipped through the sieve of her frail covalent bonds. Currently she's in the dark, the stale metallic darkness of a cash-register drawer on a Sunday morning, at the right angle of the "L" in "Legal Tender" on a five dollar bill. She's been spent, so far, on food, music, toys, sex, words.... How long will this go on? How many rounds of "birth" and "death" before our poor little polysaccharide will be released, before a more definitive death will take her? Before she'll be purified, finally, of the desire, the desperate valency that binds her to herself, and thus to the World?

Not long, writes the narrator. Because tomorrow morning, early, the narrator knows (as he knows most things that can be written) that he himself will receive this particular five-spot as change for his coffee and muffin, and later in the day, in a private but not quite meaningless little ritual—personal protest against his own acquisitiveness, his own anality and that of his culture—will *put a match* to this bit of paper, releasing her in a puff of smoke.

End of story.

Salad

On my third glass of wine, white, French, dry as a bone, everything I've shut out starts leaking in again and I hear it, hear the shrieking of grapes crushed in multitudes between the cold presses. You'd think, by this age, I'd have perfected my deafness. By what age, exactly? I'm staring across the table at my son, just now, my youngest, and he looks ancient, ancient. Cracked and drawn with many decades of stunned puzzlement. So how old does that make me? What tally of the dead, to date, have been required to keep me alive?

The fury of the panther
is in its powerlessness
before its prey.

I read that somewhere, once. Or wrote it. I was a poet, in those days. An existence I couldn't possibly have chosen. So this is the fury.

Claws are a burden. Born with them you're either a killer, or you're nothing.

Or I was a surgeon, or I dug graves.

He's brought along a salad, fresh from his own garden he claims but I'm suspicious. I suspect he hasn't got one. I suspect he lives in a featureless little cell up in the smog, like this one which seems to belong to me. Then again, how can I be certain? I'm not certain he's my youngest, that he's mine at all. We must be related in some way, though, or why would we be trapped here together, grinning foolishly at one another through this loaded silence?

Can't he hear it? The wailing of lettuce torn, the howling of peppers under the knife? To live is to live amidst carnage—to live is to kill. To feel is to feel shame. Yet there he sits, smug in his pampered body, as though he hadn't been suckled on destruction, as though he could feed on anything but despair. I want to pounce, sink my teeth into him, my gleaming, synthetic teeth. To draw blood.

I'm getting worked up again. I'm hearing my own ragged breath, nasal, whistling. I maul the air, mash molecules and suck the life out of them.

I'm a shred of sunlight gnawing at the sun.

I can't stop. Why can't I stop? When will it stop?

Corpus

I'm not sure just what you mean by a *preoccupation*. It seems to me that on the contrary I've employed a remarkably wide range of styles in my paintings, impressionism, expressionism, cubism, futurism, surrealism, and, well, and a whole bunch of other isms I can't bring to mind just now, in oils, watercolours, pastels, tempera, marine enamel, outdoor alkyd, you name it, on canvas, cardboard, masonite, and wood. And metal. And glass. And as for subject matter, I've run the gamut. Honestly, I don't see how you could ask me to be any broader. What have I left out? I've tackled religious themes, like this early one, "Cain And Abel With Vulture", and over there, "Christ In The Desert With Vulture", and my favourite in the genre, "Virgin With Vulture"—I had Mom model for Mary—not to mention mythological images, such as "Isis With Vulture", "Charybdis And Scylla With Vulture", and of course "Venus With Vulture". I've got about two dozen "Still Life With Vulture"'s. I'm sure you've seen my "Lady With Parasol And Vulture", my "Punt On The Thames With Vulture", and my "Brussels At Night With Vulture". I won an award for my colour-field piece, "Melancholy Poet With Vulture"—perhaps you heard about it? And here on the easel is my newest project, another departure for me: "Self-Portrait With Vulture".

So I hardly think it's fair to say that I'm fixated on some single theme. In fact it's all about change, for me, about transformation. I don't think I'll ever stop.

Rubber

We find this cryptic, playful pronouncement at the close of a late letter to his sister:

P.S. There is, there really is, as you saw from the start, a Creator, a prime mover, a primitive pulse that set the whole world ringing. Surprise. It's possible to reproduce this Primal Sound on any instrument by playing against that instrument, performing on it so as to reverse it, offset its idiosyncrasy (just as it's possible to witness the Creator by listening, for instance, with the eyes): by playing a drum as though it were a viola, say, a piano as though it were a piccolo, a cornet as though it were a bell. This is what I was up to, dear sister, sister dear, all those years ago when I used to sit banging with your flute on my bedroom floor....

But of course you knew that, even then, as you've known all my little "truths" before ever I massacred, mangled them with words. Never once trying to stop me....

Enough, already. Too much....

But as we see here once again, he was seeking always to stop himself, wielding a pencil just as though it were a rubber, writing just as though he were erasing.

All Possible Worlds

I've tried to understand the world, but I've not understood it. On the hot plate a can of Puss 'N Boots thickly simmers—out the window the lights of the burlesque mingle with the billion-year-old glimmer of dead stars. Glass shatters in the alley-way outside. Sounds are of struggle, stumbling feet. *Godot,* reads the writing on the wall, *—gone without you.* Like Schrödinger's cat I sit here in my black box, alive-dead, dead-alive, waiting for Jesus to peep in, for the penny to drop. Nothing happens until it's observed. What's isolated is spectre, potential. There's no body until the police get here. Work it out.

Yes, we must try to understand the world, but the world will escape us, take on brief shapes the way a stream will fill up pot holes before running on alone. Once upon a time students filled up lecture halls to hear me preach my queer theology (physics, we called it). Either everything, I explained, all worlds and all possible worlds are real, or nothing's real. Either my son is both alive and dead, or he's neither. I offered up the equations, I solved them: the universe knows when we're looking, and becomes the universe we're looking at. Naturally I lost my mind. I had the brains of a Heisenberg, of a Fa-tsang (the Buddhists knew it too, of course), but I hadn't the constitution. So, four years dead drunk, staring at a yellow wall and pissing myself. Like Bodhidharma in his cave, like my son in his coffin. Until one day, at last with nothing, I came to myself in this little room.

No one knows I'm here—to myself I'm a long-shot, a local turbulence of probability in an unlikely cosmos. I may or may not exist. Or both. Or neither. I creep out now and again to collect my cheque and my provisions, my doses of shame and flesh. Then home. Like the Zen master I shuffle about barefoot, eating when hungry, lying down when tired. Like the old cat I gaze out slit-eyed at the world, requiring neither belief nor disbelief. There's something in this of joy. My son and I were there, after all, at the Big Bang, dancing on the head of a pin. There's never been any difference.

The Tuna-Chicken Dinner isn't bad, served hot enough to scald the tongue.

In only one world am I alone. There are so many others.

Picnic

When the lion first lay down with her the lamb thought to herself, oh boy, he's going to rape me and then eat me. But the world was over—the lion was no longer in the mood. Tell me things, he said. New things, different things. Tell me what I've never heard before.

You first, said the lamb.

And so, forever, they lay side by side, whispering into one another's silky ears the perfect secrets of sweet....

Beside me you were shifting, rustling in the tall grass. The smell of passion was still on us, the smell neither of you, nor of me, nor of both of us. Rain fell out of the sky, single drops filling the single air.

I opened my mouth, tongue out, ready for my new hunger.

Acknowledgement of Sources:

Brief quotations have been drawn from the following sources: on page 11: Mishima, Yukio. *Confessions of a Mask*. New Directions, New York, 1958. (p. 39); on page 28: Brown, Norman O. *Love's Body*. Vintage, New York, 1966. (p. 99); on page 30; Robinson, James M. (ed.). *The Nag Hammadi Library*. Harper Collins, New York, 1990. (p. 126); on page 39: Mallarmé, Stéphane. *Poems*. Chatto and Windus, London, 1936. (p. 261); on page 43: Kierkegaard, Søren. *Fear and Trembling and The Sickness Unto Death*. Princeton University Press, Princeton, 1968. (p. 72); on page 64: Milisch, Harry. *The Assault*. Pantheon, New York, 1985. (p. 80); on page 66: Svevo, Italo. *Confessions of Zeno*. Vintage, New York, 1989. (p. 152); on page 67: Guibert, Hervé. *To the Friend Who Did Not Save My Life*. Atheneum, New York, 1991. (p. 47); on page 83: Bahá'u'lláh. *The Seven Valleys And The Four Valleys*. Bahá'í Publishing, Wilmette, Illinois, 1952. (p.17); on page 95: Sekida, Katsuki. *Two Zen Classics: Mumonkan And Hekiganroku*. Weatherhill, New York, 1977. (p.26); on page 102: Choron, Jacques. *Death And Western Thought*. Collier, New York, 1963. (p. 149); on page 112: Weil, Simone. *Gravity And Grace*. Routeledge, New York, 1963. (p.11); on page 113:L Pearce, Richard (ed.). *Critical Essays On Thomas Pynchon*. G.H. Hall, Boston, 1981. (p. 105).